Dear Reader,

We're thrilled that some of Harlequin's most famous families are making an encore appearance! With this special Famous Families fifty-book collection, we are proud to offer you the chance to relive the drama, the glamour, the suspense and the romance of four of Harlequin's most beloved families—the Fortunes, the Bravos, the McCabes and the Cavanaughs.

The Cavanaughs, our fourth and final family, believe in honor, justice and protecting the innocent. These values have forged a strong bond among the members of the close-knit Cavanaugh family, and make them a force to be reckoned with in the small town of Aurora, California.

The Cavanaughs do share one trait with our other famous families, though. When romance hits, all bets are off! Love changes the game for all these independent souls, turning their vulnerability into even greater strength. Prepare to be charmed by the California family created by *USA TODAY* bestselling author Marie Ferrarella.

Happy reading,

The Editors

MARIE FERRARELLA

This *USA TODAY* bestselling and RITA® Award-winning author has written more than two hundred books for Harlequin Books and Silhouette Books, some under the name Marie Nicole. Her romances are beloved by fans worldwide. Visit her website, www.marieferrarella.com.

FAMOUS FAMILIES

the CAVANAUGHS

USA TODAY Bestselling Author

MARIE FERRARELLA

The Woman Who Wasn't There

HARLEQUIN®
entertain, enrich, inspire™

To Tiffany Khauo and Eddie S. Wu.
I wish you love, now and forever.

Recycling programs
for this product may
not exist in your area.

ISBN-13: 978-0-373-36528-9

THE WOMAN WHO WASN'T THERE

Copyright © 2006 by Marie Rydzynski-Ferrarella

This edition published by arrangement with Harlequin Books S.A.

For questions and comments about the quality of this book
please contact us at CustomerService@Harlequin.com.

www.Harlequin.com

Printed in U.S.A.

FAMOUS FAMILIES

The Fortunes

Cowboy at Midnight by Ann Major
A Baby Changes Everything by Marie Ferrarella
In the Arms of the Law by Peggy Moreland
Lone Star Rancher by Laurie Paige
The Good Doctor by Karen Rose Smith
The Debutante by Elizabeth Bevarly
Keeping Her Safe by Myrna Mackenzie
The Law of Attraction by Kristi Gold
Once a Rebel by Sheri WhiteFeather
Military Man by Marie Ferrarella
Fortune's Legacy by Maureen Child
The Reckoning by Christie Ridgway

The Bravos by Christine Rimmer

The Nine-Month Marriage
Marriage by Necessity
Practically Married
Married by Accident
The Millionaire She Married
The M.D. She Had to Marry
The Marriage Agreement
The Bravo Billionaire
The Marriage Conspiracy
His Executive Sweetheart
Mercury Rising
Scrooge and the Single Girl

The McCabes by Cathy Gillen Thacker

Dr. Cowboy
Wildcat Cowboy
A Cowboy's Woman
A Cowboy Kind of Daddy
A Night Worth Remembering
The Seven-Year Proposal
The Dad Next Door
The Last Virgin in Texas
Texas Vows: A McCabe Family Saga
The Ultimate Texas Bachelor
Santa's Texas Lullaby
A Texas Wedding Vow
Blame It on Texas
A Laramie, Texas Christmas
From Texas, With Love

The Cavanaughs by Marie Ferrarella

Racing Against Time
Crime and Passion
Internal Affair
Dangerous Games
The Strong Silent Type
Cavanaugh's Woman
In Broad Daylight
Alone in the Dark
Dangerous Disguise
The Woman Who Wasn't There
Cavanaugh Watch
Cavanaugh Heat

Chapter 1

The feeling of danger threaded itself through the atmosphere, permeating every inch around her.

Pulsating.

Feeding the kernel of fear within her until it threatened to take over. The fear stole the very air away from her. She began to choke. The panic was tangible.

This isn't real. It's not real.

The words throbbed within her head, a mantra she clung to even as she felt herself cascading down the rapids of mounting terror.

And then she heard his voice. She heard it inside her head before it even reached her ears.

"Don't even think about it. Don't even *think* about running away. Don't you know you can't?" The voice mocked her without an iota of mirth. "There isn't a corner of this earth where you can run to hide from me. Not for long. Because I'll find you. And when I do, you'll learn what it means to cross me.

"I could shred the very skin off your bones and no one'll lift a finger to help you. No one'll lift a finger against me.

"Do you understand?"

The words, disembodied, branded her soul.

She couldn't see him. Only feel his hot breath, tinged with alcohol and malice, along her skin. Along her face, her neck, down to her very toes. It burned.

He was right. There was nowhere to run. Nowhere to hide. She was vulnerable. Naked before him as she always was now. In spirit if not in fact.

But it was her spirit that kept her going. The spirit, the courage she'd found deep within her. The spirit he'd tried to rip from her. Grasping it like a solid entity in her hands, she fled. Fled as she was bound to. Because she knew if she stayed, somehow, some way, she'd be dead. He'd see to that. She knew it as well as she knew her own name.

So she ran.

Ran until her lungs ached and her legs threatened to give out beneath her. And then she ran some more. And always, always, she felt his presence right there behind her. Felt it even though she couldn't see it.

Then suddenly he was there, grabbing her. His two hands wound around her throat and he was choking her. Making the air disappear again.

Even though she still couldn't see him, his eyes were

gleaming above her as his thumbs applied pressure on her windpipe.

"You're mine. You'll always be mine. Mine."

Delene D'Angelo bolted upright in her bed. It took her a moment to realize that the shrieking that had woken her up came from her. She pressed her trembling fingers over her mouth to still the noise.

She couldn't still the trembling.

It was March. March in the Northern California city of Aurora was still fairly cold, but she was sweating. Her short platinum-blond hair was plastered against her forehead, and the jersey she slept in, the single habit that tied her to her past, adhered to her body as if she'd just been shoved into the center of a pool.

Her body was slick with the perspiration of fear. She threaded her arms around herself and rocked, the motion comforting her only a little.

The sound of her labored breathing filled the small, sparsely furnished loft apartment. Delene did her best to regulate it. To still it as she strained to listen.

Were there any other sounds in the room, hidden by the noise she made? She caught her breath, even though it hurt her lungs. She still felt as if she'd run a long distance. And she had. She'd run for five years.

There was no other sound in the room. The tiny rented apartment was silent.

Like a house of cards, Delene collapsed, her head falling forward for a moment to lean against her clenched knees. After a moment, she began to pull herself together. Taking a deep, cleansing breath, she dragged her hand through her hair.

It was a dream. A nightmare.

Again.

She made a small, disparaging noise in the darkness, shaking her head. Was she ever going to be free of them? Or were they—was it—going to haunt her forever?

It had been five years, five long years, since she'd walked into this brand-new life she'd laid out for herself. Five years since she'd fled from the other world she'd inhabited. When would the nightmares finally leave her alone? When would she stop looking over her shoulder, wondering if that noise she heard was harmless, or if it was a warning to run?

The nightmares assaulted her three, sometimes four times a week. Granted, that was less frequent than before. But just marginally. When she had first escaped, she'd have the nightmares every night. Whenever she closed her eyes, there was her old life, waiting for her. Mocking her.

And there he stood. Russell. Looming larger than life. Grabbing at her. Capturing her again.

"A dream, Dee. Just a dream," she told herself out loud, her voice harsh and stern as if she were trying to snap someone out of succumbing to hysteria.

She could feel the tears that wanted to come and she banished them. Tears were worse than useless. They were a sign of weakness, and she couldn't afford to be weak. Not even for a moment.

Delene sat there in the dark, willing herself into a state of rational calm.

"Maybe I should go to a shrink. Have someone help me get these thoughts out of my head."

Her words skimmed along the shadows. It was just talk. She wasn't about to expose her fears to anyone. Didn't really trust anyone enough to talk to them. She couldn't risk it. Because Russell and the people he worked for had eyes and ears everywhere and somehow it would get back to him.

And then he'd have her. And kill her. Just as he'd threatened he would. He wasn't given to making idle threats. That wasn't his style. And style was everything to Russell. That and his reputation.

Delene shifted, swinging her legs out of the double bed. She sat for a moment, staring into the semidarkness, the chill in the air slowly creeping over her. After a beat, she blew out a breath.

Her breathing was almost steady. And her pulse was slowing down to something considerably less than the speed of sound.

She was going to be all right.

Until the next time.

Glancing at the clock on her nightstand, Delene rotated her shoulders, throwing off the last remnants of sleep that might have still been clinging to her body if not her mind. The bright blue numbers on the clock registered in her brain. Four o'clock. An ungodly hour for everyone but bakers and a handful of medical professionals. And her. It was time for her to be getting up today.

There was a raid she was scheduled to conduct.

Less than half an hour later, Delene finished buttoning the khaki-colored blouse and slipped the ends inside similar-colored slacks. Her mouth quirked at her reflection. She certainly didn't look like someone who was plagued by nightmares. Or someone who diligently checked the locks on her windows and door first thing every morning as soon as her feet hit the floor. And the last thing every night before she went to bed.

She'd learned to install the locks herself rather than trusting someone else to do it for her. Locks to keep the source of her nightmare out.

Given her past, she hadn't exactly picked a profession that was designed to give her peace of mind. But it was the last kind of career Russell would think she'd become involved in, so she'd taken to it like a duck to water.

She was glad to finally make use of her degree for something. Eye candy had no use for a degree in criminology. And the idea of her working at anything had displeased Russell.

Her present career served as an outlet for her on more than one level. She was a probation officer for the county, had been for five years, thanks to a little altering of her school records by a friend. The education hadn't been a lie, only the name in the records.

Being a probation officer allowed her to do something positive. It gave her the opportunity to help the people who genuinely wanted to atone for their transgressions and get on with their lives. To make something of themselves by putting their lives on a different track. The way she ultimately had.

And it also allowed her to keep tabs on the people who had thought that somehow they'd beaten the system and received a "get out of jail" card for nothing. The ones who felt they were invincible. Those she took special pleasure in foiling.

And each time she did, she thought of Russell. Of how it would feel to send him to prison. This empowered her.

That was what this morning's raid was all about—checking up on one of her charges. Clyde Petrie was a mean-mouthed, small-time drug dealer who'd gotten a walk the first time because of a technicality and a slap on the wrist plus probation for dealing the second time. Both times he'd gotten lucky and drawn judges who believed he could be rehabilitated. Both Judge Walker and Judge Le felt that space in the overcrowded jails should be saved for the truly hardened criminals, the ones who raped and maimed their victims before killing them. To them, Clyde was just an annoying gnat to be swatted away.

Thinking himself in possession of a charmed life, or maybe just too stupid to learn from his mistakes, Clyde had gone back to doing what he did best. Dealing. And this time, it might result in his undoing. But Clyde, when faced with the threat of serious jail time, had blurted out that he had something to trade. Something big. He'd singled Delene out, begged her to be his advocate and she in turn had brought the matter to the court-appointed lawyer. The latter had concurred.

Against the better judgment of the assistant district attorney who oversaw the case, Clyde had somehow managed to get out on bail. But he was still on the books as one of her cases, and until he was either under lock and key, or in protective custody, she intended to keep tabs on him. To keep him as straight as possible.

One of the best ways was to conduct a raid. Probation officers had the right to turn up in the dead of night on the person's doorstep, demanding entry. They could legally toss his or her possessions to make sure that there were no illegal substances or weapons on the premises. Fear of jail was supposed to keep them honest.

However, this raid was just a cover. To establish an alibi for Clyde and throw suspicion off—until he testified against the man who ultimately gave him his supply, one Miguel Mendoza.

Delene put the cereal bowl she'd only half filled into the sink, running water into it. Then she checked her weapon, the way she did every morning. In the five years she'd owned the gun, she'd never fired it in the line of duty and didn't intend to.

Unless Russell found her.

Satisfied as to its condition, she holstered her weapon. She was ready.

Once Clyde said what he had to say at Mendoza's

trial, the government would give him a new identity and send him off to some obscure location. Where he would undoubtedly run afoul of law, Delene thought grimly. Someone like Clyde seemed predisposed to stumble. But that wasn't her concern. She had to make sure the case closed satisfactorily. In this instance, getting Clyde into court to testify and then into the hands of another branch of the government, who would take it from there.

Her hair still slightly damp from the quick shower she'd taken, Delene got in behind the wheel of her small, nondescript vehicle. She liked it better than the Jaguar she'd driven in her other life, because the Jaguar had been a symbol of her servitude. This second-hand car, bought with her own money, was a symbol of her independence.

After buckling up, she turned on the rebuilt engine the department mechanic had installed for her at cost, and switched on the lights. The mechanic, a twenty-year veteran with the department, had taken pity on her when the car had all but died at his feet. He told her she reminded him of his youngest daughter. She'd still kept her guard up. It grew tiring at times.

Pulling out of the carport, Delene drove toward the Traveler's Motel, a seedy little place comprised of eighteen units, all in need of some kind of repair. Clyde called it home when he wasn't cooling his heels in a holding tank. She was meeting Adrian Jones and Jorge O'Reilly there, the two men joining her in the raid.

Dawn was still more than an hour away.

* * *

"Oh, damn."

Standing to her right, Adrian nodded. Tall, athletic and given to grinning, he sported a grim smile now as he said, "Yup, I'd say that about sums it up."

They, along with Jorge, found themselves looking down at the body that lay facedown in the middle of a flattened rug. The floor covering had long since lost any hint of an actual color. Its present hue was a combination of over a decade's worth of stains and dirt. At the moment, its most prominent color was provided by the pool of blood slowly darkening as it was drying. The blood, until recently, had been part of Clyde Petrie's limited supply.

The county's only witness against Miguel Mendoza was dead.

Moments earlier, on Delene's order, Jorge had applied his considerable bulk to the front door, taking it down after several quick raps went unreplied. It had made Delene somewhat uneasy that there hadn't been the sound of scurrying on the other side of the door to indicate the quick disposal of drugs or some other illegal contraband. That was when she'd given Jorge the signal for a quick entry.

They'd stumbled over Clyde's body the second they'd gained admittance.

The heat was on, causing the ripening smell of death to take possession of the single-room unit. Taking a breath to steel herself, Delene leaned over and checked Clyde's neck for a pulse just in case he'd managed to continue his lucky streak. His luck had apparently run out when he needed it most. There was no pulse.

"Looks like Mendoza got to him first," Jorge surmised. He loosened his collar. Despite the open door, it felt stuffy in the room.

She got to her feet, ignoring the hand the large man offered her. Not because of any disdain she felt, because she didn't. She got along as well as could be expected with the two men. They were pleasant and decent. But she was stubbornly determined to do everything for herself and accept no help unless she absolutely had to. The less dependent she was on anyone, the safer she was. That meant building no bridges, forging no relationships beyond the office.

As far as coworkers went, both Adrian and Jorge were good men. They were both likable, both married and Jorge had two kids with one on the way. And more importantly, they didn't look down on her for being a female in what could be easily thought of as a man's world. They treated her like a person and she was grateful for that. But not grateful enough to think of either man as a friend.

She sighed, shaking her head. Thinking of the waste. Clyde had been safer in jail than in the place he called home.

"Looks like," she agreed. The logical conclusion was that Miguel Mendoza, the former gang member who'd risen up to become a drug lord of some consequence, had eliminated their star witness.

But Delene knew nothing was ever so crystal clear.

If it was, she would still be in Colorado.

Taking her cell phone out of her hip pocket, she dialed the number that would connect her to their liaison in the police department. As it rang, she looked at the body on the floor. Clyde Petrie was no longer her concern. Technically.

"You've just got to get a bigger car."

The words were grunted out as Troy Cavanaugh, the last of Brian Cavanaugh's sons to make detective, folded his six-foot-three frame into the vehicle he swore was a subcompact. It wasn't the first time he'd made the complaint to Kara Ward, the homicide detective the department had paired him with almost immediately after awarding him his gold shield.

As before, Kara sniffed at his words. The vehicle was a perfect fit for her, but then, she was only five-one in her bare feet. As far as he was concerned, that wasn't even people-sized. She could have just as easily ridden around in a toy car. But he needed something with space, and Kara's car was cutting off the circulation to the lower half of his body.

Kara gave him a look that said beggars had no right to be choosers—or complainers.

"Either that or a partner who can't pass as a float in the Thanksgiving Day parade," the woman quipped. She watched as he struggled to buckle up. "Not my fault you didn't have the good sense to know when you should stop growing."

Troy shook his head. Or attempted to. The car wasn't

much on head room, either. The one he normally rode in—the one he drove—was currently in the shop after a rather damaging encounter with a fire hydrant. Said encounter was the result of the tail end of a high-speed chase with a man suspected of killing his pregnant girl-friend to keep her from talking to his wife. The chase had ended in the man's apprehension as well as the wrecked car and a substantial repair bill—both for the car and the fire hydrant.

All this had happened yesterday and Troy hadn't gotten a chance to get a replacement. When the call had come in this morning, taking him away from a rather pleasant dream, he'd had no choice but to agree to have Kara come pick him up. Something he'd regretted the moment he'd hung up the phone.

Finally he managed to get the metal end of the seat belt into the slot. There was a stitch in his side.

"I'm going to the car rental agency after work," he announced, trying to sit straight. It was a futile attempt. "Get a real vehicle instead of a clown car."

Kara glanced toward him. "Keep this up and I won't let you have the can opener you'll need to get out of this one when we get to the motel."

Taking a corner sharply, she laughed at the stifled curse coming from the passenger side. A minute later, they were pulling up into the parking lot of the motel. Kara smoothly parked her pride and joy next to a large white van with blue and green lettering across the side. The sign proclaimed it to be a crime scene investigation vehicle for the city of Aurora.

Bracing one hand on the dashboard and one on the roof of the compact, Troy managed to extract himself from the torturous vehicle, although it wasn't easy. His partner hadn't left all that much space for him on his side. Straightening, he fixed his jacket.

"Looks like the CSI people got here ahead of us," he noted.

Kara laughed shortly as she closed her door. "Easy to see how you earned your shield."

One of four siblings with seven cousins, most of whom were older, Troy had learned early on to roll with the punches and take things lightly. It was the key to survival. He grinned at Kara as they made their way to the motel room.

"What's up, Kara? Your hot-and-heavy date decide to hog the covers?"

She frowned as she gave him a dirty look. "None of your business what my hot-and-heavy date did with the covers." The next moment she offered a somewhat lukewarm apology. "Sorry, Cavanaugh. Didn't mean to snap at you."

"Yeah, you did." As he spoke, he looked around at the area. Light was uncharitable to the motel, exposing all its dingy, dirty little secrets. "But that's okay. I've got a sister who's pretty much as even-tempered as you are. Rolls right off my back."

Kara snorted. "Remind me to send condolences to your sister."

"Funny—" Troy opened the door to the motel room

and moved back to let Kara enter first "—I was thinking the same thing about your hot-and-heavy date."

The room was like every other run-down motel room that littered not only this state, but every other one, as well. In its own way, the space bore the mark of the countless people who had passed through over the years, leaving not only the stench of hopelessness in their wake, but a coat of grime that went down too many layers to clean.

Ordinarily, the first thing Troy took in when he entered a crime scene was the reason for his presence: the victim. But this time, his attention was momentarily drawn to the three people who were standing off to the side, conferring with one of the crime scene investigators. There were two men and a woman, identically dressed in the uniform provided by the county's probation department. They couldn't have been more different. One man was tall and thin, the other shorter and far more heavyset.

But it was the woman who captured his attention. Not because she was the only female in the trio, but because her delicate features seemed so out of place, so alien to the drab uniform she was wore. The clothing belonged to someone who was hardened, someone accustomed to dealing with the dregs of society.

She, on the other hand, looked like someone who might have inspired a Renaissance artist to go run for his paints and his brush in an effort to somehow capture this vision of an angel walking the earth.

"Hey, Cavanaugh," Kara whispered, "you're staring.

Get your tongue back in your head before you wind up embarrassing me."

"Too late for that, Kara," Troy heard himself whispering back, only half-aware that he was even answering her. "They've already seen you."

Kara muttered something cryptic and sarcastic in response, but her words just formed a slight buzz in the background.

He and the woman in the probation officer's uniform had just made eye contact and he had to remind himself to breathe.

The only problem was he'd forgotten how.

Chapter 2

He was staring at her.

Did the man who'd just walked into room know her? Recognize her from somewhere? Delene thought he looked familiar, but she couldn't be sure.

Long, thin, spidery fingers of panic skittered through her as she struggled to place the tall, dark man in the black slacks and equally black turtleneck sweater he wore beneath a blue windbreaker.

This was stupid.

Annoyed with herself, Delene banked down the growing fear. She was overreacting again. It was obvious by his manner, by the way he took over a room, that he was a police detective. And since she was an agent with the County Probation Department, more than likely their paths had crossed once, if not several times. So he was probably just trying to place her. There, a logical explanation. No big deal.

Delene did her best to stifle an impatient sigh. The impatience was directed at herself. How long was it going to take before she felt safe? Before a look was just a look and not the outward sign of pending exposure? Of a reason to run? She wished she could say soon, but she knew better.

Squaring her shoulders, she ran her fingers through her short hair, pushing it away from her face as she donned her "go-to-hell" attitude, the one that had kept her secure up to now. She looked straight at the tall, dark-haired man with the penetrating blue eyes, wicked smile and cleft chin.

"Something I can do for you, Detective?"

The woman who'd caught his attention had a voice like smooth, fine wine, aged to perfection. It slid over him, warming him as it wove its path.

Lots of things come to mind, lady.

Outgoing and gregarious, Troy still possessed a healthy dose of prudence. Rather than allow them to be heard, he kept the words that instantly rose to his lips safely locked away in his head. He and the woman were in mixed company and he had no idea how the blond vision in the bland uniform might react to an honest response her question had generated. He never forgot whose son he was. The weight of the family name was not something he bore lightly. So far, none of the Cavanaugh men had ever been accused of verbal sexual harassment, however unintentional. He didn't intend to be the first.

So instead of saying what was on his mind and seeing where it might lead, he buried his curiosity and followed protocol. That meant asking questions and making noises like a homicide detective. "You the first one on the scene?"

Delene gestured to the two men on either side of her. "All three of us were."

Troy looked at the men, particularly the older of the two. The one built like an armored tank. He glanced over his shoulder at the doorway before commenting. "Must have been a tight fit."

She took immediate exception at his light tone, thinking it a dig against Jorge. She didn't like an outsider making fun of the man.

Her answer was crisp, putting distance between them. "Jorge took down the door. For all intents and purposes, we came in together." She nodded toward the body on the rug. "We found him like this."

Troy nodded thoughtfully. "And why were you looking for him?"

Out of the corner of his eye, he could see Kara make her way over to the crime scene investigator. She was going to get the man's take on the evidence he'd discovered and processed so far.

Despite coming from two very different places in life, and Kara's obvious initial preconceived notions about how he had risen up so quickly through the ranks, they worked well together. Divide and conquer was the way they approached a case. So far, neither one of them had any real complaints about the other. Aside from a very short sizing-up period, there'd been no attempt to establish territory, no squabbling about which of them was to be the top dog. They operated as a team.

"Standard procedure," Adrian told him, cutting in. It was obvious to Troy that the taller of the two men was feeling somewhat protective of the woman. "We were conducting an early morning raid." When Troy looked at him for further elaboration, he added, "Just to make sure his *i*'s were dotted and his *t*'s were crossed."

Troy frowned, eyeing the pathetic shell of a man on the floor. "I don't know about his *i*'s and his *t*'s, but I've got a hunch he wasn't looking to get a bullet in his head."

After taking plastic gloves out of his pocket, Troy put them on, then squatted down beside the body. Very gently he lifted the victim's head. He examined the point of entry, then looked to see if there was an exit wound. There wasn't.

"A bullet he seems to be hanging on to." More for the medical examiner to do, he thought as he placed Clyde's head back down in the position he'd found it. Behind him he heard a sharp intake of breath.

"I'm not through in here, yet," CSI Sam Connor said waspishly. By his expression, it was evident Sam thought of the body as his property.

On his feet again, Troy raised his gloved hands in the air, silently showing the man that he was no longer touching the body. Because he'd gotten what appeared to be a drop of blood on one of the gloves, Troy stripped them off and rolled the tainted one inside of the second glove before putting both in his pocket.

"How about you?" He directed the question and his eyes back to the woman from the county. "Are you through here yet, Officer..." Troy paused, reading the neat little letters affixed over the woman's breast pocket. He lingered, longer than he should have, taking in the very enticing, very inviting swell of her full chest before raising his eyes to her face. "D'Angelo," he concluded.

Delene glanced at the man whose lifeless body was now surrounded by a chalk outline. Pity tugged at her heart. In the final analysis, she felt sorry for the dead man she'd interacted with a handful of times. Clyde had been a lower life-form, but he'd still been a human being, and as such, didn't deserve to be so casually eliminated. She doubted if his executioner had even given his death so much as a passing thought.

If he'd been killed by whom she thought he'd been killed, it was in part her fault. But mostly Clyde's.

She nodded in reply to the detective's question. "He's way past caring about anything we might find in the motel room that might be in violation of his probation."

Was that emotion he heard in her voice? Her expression remained steely. Troy decided he'd imagined the trace of sorrow. He shook his head as he looked at the victim. There appeared to be no signs of struggle. The messy room seemed to be just that, a messy room. Probably never even knew what hit him, Troy thought.

"Really must have ticked someone off," he commented, then looked at the probation officers, his glance sweeping over all three. "Any ideas?"

The question surprised Delene. All the detectives she'd ever come across in this job acted as if they'd been first in line when brains had been handed out and everyone else had been a distant second, if not third or fourth. They rarely asked for opinions, preferring to come up with their own.

Slipping her hands into her back pockets, she thought of the daughter Clyde had once admitted to her that he'd fathered. The girl, Rachel, was about four or five now. She deserved to know that her father was gone. Trouble was, Delene had no idea how to find the girl and her mother.

"You might think about sending someone to question Miguel Mendoza," she finally told the detective.

Troy raised his eyebrows at the familiar name. "*The* Miguel Mendoza?"

When the woman nodded, saying nothing further, Troy asked, "Why?" He'd assumed the dead man was just a junkie. There were track marks on his arms. To say that Mendoza might have a hand in it meant that the victim hadn't just been on the receiving end of drugs, he'd been pushing them, as well. "This guy caught skimming?"

The moment he said it, the suggestion seemed ludicrous. Troy looked around at the dead man's living conditions. Fast-food wrappers littered various corners of the room, clothes beyond dirty discarded beside them.

If the dead man had been keeping some of the money he made pushing drugs, he had to have used it to buy more drugs for himself. It had certainly not been used to better his lifestyle.

Delene paused before answering. The police detective with the broad shoulders and his much shorter partner seemed perfectly capable of doing their own legwork, chasing down their own leads. But she saw no harm in sharing information. Clyde's deal with the D.A. would come out soon enough, even if her part wouldn't. She doubted if the D.A. had noted down that she had been the one to ultimately convince Clyde to turn a corner and try to make something of himself for his daughter's sake. She felt it was part of her job, to help rehabilitate those who had a spark of potential for leading an honest life.

Delene glanced up at the detective with the engaging smile. He hadn't just dismissed her and her team as being annoying and in the way. He'd spoken to her, to them, as if they were all on the same side. So for the moment she would be.

"Clyde was going to testify against Mendoza in court."

"Clyde?" Troy looked at the inert body, trying to picture the man responding to the name. He didn't look like a Clyde. He didn't look very much like anything at all. Except dead.

"Clyde Petrie," Delene provided. "He was involved with drugs since he was fourteen. At seventeen he dropped out of school, thought he'd make a better living for himself by pushing drugs instead of doing something that his high school diploma might land him. He was picked up twice for dealing. Managed to elude jail both times. Second time landed him on probation. It made him feel lucky."

Which had been Clyde's downfall, she thought. Thinking herself lucky had been hers, as well. She'd thought herself lucky to have caught Russell's eye. Nothing could have been further from the truth.

"Third time was the charm for the county. This time the judge wasn't going to let him slide," she continued. "He was going to get sent away for the maximum."

"But he got another stab at probation," Troy guessed, from her presence. "Why?" And then, before the woman or her companions could answer, he remembered what she'd said at the beginning. "Because he made a deal to give evidence against Mendoza in open court."

"You're quick."

There was no missing the sarcasm in the woman's voice. But Troy played it straight. He glanced in Kara's direction. His partner had just looked up and their eyes met. "Rubs off from the company I keep."

He was rewarded with a wide grin and a chuckle, both from Kara. His brothers had taught him that it never hurt to have your partner in a good mood.

Delene drew her own conclusions from the quick exchange between the duo. The detectives were sleeping together, she guessed. She never knew a good-looking man who didn't try to take advantage of his looks. The homely ones took a little longer to come up for their turn at bat. But they always came.

She frowned. "Whatever."

Already she was trying to distance herself from the scene. From the man who lay dead on the floor. She wished she could view the individuals she dealt with as just case files, the way Jorge did. He'd told her she'd be a lot better off that way, and she didn't doubt it. But detaching herself would also mean surrendering the last bit of humanity she still possessed.

"Might be off base entirely," Delene continued. "But you might find that Mendoza's worth a look."

And so was she, Troy thought. A look, a gaze, an out-and-out, clock-stopping stare. The longer he looked at her face, the more flawless it seemed.

And the more out of place the woman appeared at the scene.

What was her story? he wondered. What was she doing, banging on motel doors before dawn, trying to raise the dead and defiant, not to mention the dregs of society? Without her uniform, she belonged in a pure, pristine setting.

Especially without her uniform on, he thought, doing his best to suppress the smile that fought to curve his mouth.

"Mendoza. Absolutely," he agreed, realizing that he *had* been staring. He cleared his throat, as if that would erase the awkward moment. "Where can I get in touch with you?" When she didn't answer, he added, "If I have more questions?"

"Probation office." The answer came from the armored tank at her side as the man put his bulk in between his petite team leader and the tall detective. Almost grudgingly, Jorge offered up a cream-colored business card with the probation department's main office's phone number. The small card appeared that much smaller when contrasted against his wide, powerful, deeply tanned hand.

Troy took the card, raising his eyes to the woman's beefy protector. One side of his mouth lifted in a lopsided, amused smile. He'd had no idea that guardian angels came in the extralarge size. "Thanks, Jorge."

Jorge's expression never changed, never softened. "Officer O'Reilly," he corrected. "Or Agent O'Reilly, if you prefer."

So much for law enforcement being one big, happy family, Troy thought.

"And for the record, I'm Adrian Jones," the tall man told him.

Jorge and Adrian, Cinderella's two ugly stepsisters, Troy couldn't help labeling them as the two men flanked—and all but towered over—the delicate blonde. Except that in this case, Cinderella's stepsisters were highly protective of her.

"We'd better get going," Delene said to the two men with her.

There was no point in their hanging around. She didn't relish making this report to the head of the department. Or calling the D.A. for that matter. She knew that the detectives would probably take care of it, but she'd been the one to make the initial suggestion to the D.A., letting him know about Clyde's connection to Mendoza. Taking pity on Clyde.

Look where her pity had gotten him.

"And just for the record," Troy called after the woman just as she and the two men began to file out, "what's your first name?"

"I think he means you," Jorge growled. "Want me to take care of it?"

Delene shook her head, then glanced at the detective. "Something you don't need to know," she told him just as she began to walk out the door.

Troy raised his voice. "I'll need a full statement."

"You'll get it," she promised. "After I give it to my boss." With that, she exited. Jorge and Adrian followed.

Approaching Troy, Kara made a series of small, undefinable noises that indicated her enjoyment of what had just transpired. "Well, she sure put you in your place, didn't she?" Kara laughed.

"Did she?" Troy murmured, getting down to work. "I hadn't noticed."

But he was going to make Agent D'Angelo sit up and take notice. He was never one to walk away from a challenge, and everything about the petite blonde had been a challenge.

"Why haven't you hit on me, Cavanaugh?"

The question came without any preamble, moments after Troy had once more stuffed himself into his partner's torture chamber of a car. He was busy counting the seconds until they reached the precinct, trying to ignore the very real pain in his back. Two minutes into the ride and his legs were a lost cause.

"Right now I'm seriously thinking of just hitting you for letting yourself get talked into buying a car left over from the Spanish Inquisition," Troy muttered, more to himself than to her.

And then as her question penetrated, he looked at his partner. She slowed her vehicle to a stop at the first light they reached. Kara Ward was a lively, attractive woman with a pretty face and a sharp mind. But he thought of her as he thought of Janelle. As a sister. They had chemistry, but as partners, not as a man and a woman.

"Why?" he asked, uttering his words slowly. "Would you like me to hit on you?"

She lifted a single shoulder in a dismissive shrug. The light turned green and she shifted her foot onto the gas pedal. "I'd like to feel you thought I was worth the effort."

Since he loathed getting into any kind of physical altercations, diplomacy had become second nature to him.

"Kara, you are very much worth the effort," he assured her with warmth. "But what we have now works, and if I hit on you and somewhere down the line you decide that you don't want any part of me—" he was careful to make it seem like all the choices were hers "—where would that leave us? Looking for other partners. Partners who might not be as in tune to us as we are to each other. So, for the sake of work relations, I don't act on any impulses I might have about you."

She slanted a glance at him, not quite buying into what he was selling, but playing along for the fun of it. "But you do have impulses about me."

He offered her his most solemn expression. "All the time."

Kara was no more a fool than Troy was. "Oh, really?"

"Scout's honor." If he could have managed it, he would have raised one hand up in the scout salute, but his hands were tucked against his chest, lodged in by his knees. Early Christian martyrs had been more comfortable than he was.

After taking a corner, she eyed him again, her mouth curving. "And you just bank them down?"

"Yup." He tried to take a deep breath and found that he couldn't. His knees were keeping his chest from expanding. "Plus, I take a lot of cold showers."

She laughed. "Good answer." With a sweeping turn of the steering wheel, Kara pulled her vehicle into the precinct's parking lot and guided it to a spot in the second row.

After getting out, she rounded the all-but-nonexistent hood and came over to his side, opening the door for him. "Need help getting out?"

Troy ignored the smirk on her face. "Just find me the name of the rental agency the department uses," he told Kara, then gritted his teeth as he maneuvered out of the death grip the passenger seat had on him.

* * *

"You think he was good-looking?"

They'd all pulled into the county's probation department's parking lot at the same time and walked into the building together. Jorge had waited until they stepped out of the elevator before asking Delene his question.

Preoccupied thinking about Clyde and the phone call she was going to have to make to the D.A., Delene didn't immediately follow Jorge's line of thinking. "Who?"

Jorge frowned. "That pretty boy at the motel."

Delene looked up at him innocently before entering the general office. "Clyde?"

"No, not Clyde," Adrian put in impatiently, backing up Jorge. "That detective. Cavanaugh."

"Cavanaugh?" Delene rolled the name over on her tongue. The man hadn't shown them any credentials. "Was that his name?"

"Yeah, heard he was the chief of detectives' son. One of them anyway," Adrian corrected, frowning. He pushed the door open for Delene. "Cavanaughs move around that precinct as if they owned it."

Jorge snorted. "With eleven of them in the department, they might as well own it."

"Eleven?" she asked in surprise. The disdainful note in Jorge's voice was not lost on her. And it did make her wonder. There were twenty-one in Jorge's family. He was the last person she would have thought to be critical of large families.

"No, not eleven," Adrian corrected. "Nine." There

were nine Cavanaugh detectives on the force, three of them female. "Not counting the chief of detectives."

Jorge paused, then asked, "What about the old man?"

Delene glanced from one man to the other. "What old man?"

"The chief of police," Jorge told her. "Andrew Cavanaugh."

"He's not there anymore," Adrian reminded him. "Retired some years back. He doesn't count."

They entered the large bull pen that comprised their office. Cubicles divided up the area as far as the eye could see.

"Try telling that to one of his relatives," Jorge interjected.

The conversation went on, doing very well without any input from her. But something Jorge had just said made her think. And wonder wistfully, if just for the moment, what it had to be like to be part of a large family, instead of alone and on the run.

It wasn't something she figured she'd ever find out firsthand.

Burying her thoughts, she went to her cubicle to make that call she was dreading. The one to the D.A.

Chapter 3

Clyde Petrie's body had long been officially pronounced dead, tagged and removed. All that was left to mark the passage of his life was a chalk outline on the rug, a dried pool of blood that had gone outside the lines and several piles of greasy fast-food wrappers.

The room was quiet, even if the surrounding area was not. Muffled voices came from the next unit. Whether they were coming from people or a television set, Troy wasn't sure. It didn't matter. He blocked out the sound.

Wearing pale plastic gloves, Troy switched on the light. Rather than illuminate, it added to the overall sense of darkness and gloom within the room.

He was grateful he'd had the good fortune to be born into the life that he presently enjoyed.

Squatting down beside the pile closest to the door, Troy began poking through the crumbled papers, crushed paper cups and greasy bags. He was searching for that certain "something" they might have overlooked when they'd first gone through this room hours ago. The "something" that just possibly might be able to lead them to the penny-ante dealer's killer when all the obvious trails led nowhere.

All it took was one thing. That serial killer in New York back in the seventies had been caught because of unpaid parking tickets, Troy mused, working his way to the floor. Anything was possible.

Besides, he did some of his best work when it was quiet. When he could think. He and Kara had conducted a canvas of the area and now she and her clown car were back at the squad room, following up on information given by the woman who lived across the parking lot. After an intense two hours, Sam, the crime scene investigator, had retreated to his lab with his odd collection of fibers, cigarette butts and whatever to examine, tag and match.

Troy glanced at the watch his father had given him when he'd graduated from the academy. Right about now the M.E. was taking the victim apart. Literally.

Troy rose, absently dusting off one gloved hand against another as he scanned the room. More than sifting through the dead dealer's possessions, he was trying to fit into the man's emaciated skin. To think the way Clyde might have thought in the last few hours of his life. And maybe, just maybe, he was also trying to prove to the world at large that he wasn't just chief of detectives Brian Cavanaugh's youngest, indulged son.

He was proud of who he was, who he belonged to. The Cavanaugh name stood for something in Aurora, but there was no denying that it also carried a significant weight with it. You couldn't really slack off if you were a Cavanaugh. At least, not for very long. People expected you to behave as if you were a little larger than life. Of course, some were waiting to see if you fell on your face.

He had no intention of falling. He had brothers and cousins to compete against, he always had.

Troy walked over to the closet and opened the door. It creaked. More fast-food wrappers were inside, as if Clyde had actually made a halfhearted attempt at cleaning his living quarters before giving up.

"Would have been easier to throw it all away, Clyde," he said under his breath. He began to move around the wrappers, one by one.

Granted, the competition between him and the other members of his family was a friendly one, but he still had to prove himself. He was the youngest of the Cavanaugh men. Only his sister and Rayne, Uncle Andrew's daughter, were younger, and not by all that much. There was a stigma attached to being the youngest. Family didn't really expect you to measure up.

Though he never said it out loud, sometimes didn't even admit it to himself, he wanted to make his father proud. Wanted the whole family to be proud of him. The only way that happened—to his satisfaction—was to be the best damn cop, the best damn detective he knew how.

He knew that his family would love him, would stick by him no matter what he did. But he had seen that look of pride rise up in his father's eyes when he'd told him that he was going into "the family business" and becoming a cop, the way the rest of them had. The way his father, Uncle Andrew and Uncle Mike had, following in their father's footsteps. It was a look he wanted to see over and over again.

The sudden, small noise behind him had Troy whirling around, his gun instantly drawn. Aimed.

The next moment, blowing out a breath, he raised the gun's barrel up toward the ceiling, putting the safety back on.

Though her expression never gave her away, Delene could feel her racing heart slowly sliding down from her throat.

"How many hours of practice did it take you to get that fast?" She lowered the hands that she'd automatically raised the second he'd pointed the gun at her. Leaving the doorway, she crossed into the room.

Saying something unintelligible under his breath, Troy holstered his weapon, then readjusted his windbreaker over it.

"Enough," he replied, then asked a question of his own. "What are you doing here?" She'd left here hours ago and had no authority to be in the motel room. It was still a crime scene. "Forget something?"

For a second, Delene debated retracing her steps and

leaving. She could always come back later tonight. She knew how to bypass locks. One of the fringe benefits of her earlier life. But to leave now would mean that she'd allowed someone to chase her off, and that just wasn't going to happen. That, too, belonged to her past.

She slowly shook her head. "No, I'm looking for something."

Troy's dark eyebrows drew together over his nose in a puzzled, wavy line. Talking wasn't this woman's strong suit, he decided. Considering what he was accustomed to from the women in his family, reticence was a pleasant change. But not when he wanted information. "Mind telling me what?"

Yes, she minded, Delene thought. She minded having to explain herself to anyone. It brought back too many bad memories. She was trying to forget about endless months of explaining herself, of justifying every move she made, every second she was away from the house.

But Detective Cavanaugh wasn't asking out of personal curiosity. This was all part of his job.

"You did see the yellow tape, didn't you?" Troy prompted when she didn't immediately respond.

Delene could feel that old familiar flash of temper coming on. "Vision's twenty-twenty the last time I had my eyes checked."

The flippant answer was as mechanical as breathing for her. Being flippant was the defense mechanism Delene employed to keep people from asking her too many probing questions. She banked down a lot of other words, as well. After all, the man was just doing his job.

And what you're doing is going above and beyond the call of duty. But she knew she had to at least try, she thought.

There was more to the woman's eyes than twenty-twenty vision, Troy caught himself observing. Her eyes were a deep, dark shade of green. So green, he felt as if he'd fallen into the center of an emerald mine. So green that they could very easily mesmerize him and dissolve his thoughts if he allowed it.

Troy cleared his throat. "Nice to know. But you still haven't answered my question."

Her mouth rose in an amused smile that took him prisoner. "I thought you gave me a choice."

He didn't follow. "A choice?"

"Yes." She raised her head to look up at him. "You said, 'Mind telling me what?' That would indicate if I do mind, I don't have to answer you."

Troy moved in a little closer, although he wasn't completely aware that he had taken a step. She liked to argue. Maybe she wasn't all that different from the women in his family.

"Which automatically puts you on my list of people to look at more closely."

The way he said it, Delene got the distinct feeling the detective wasn't just talking about the murder. That he meant something more intimate than that.

For just the barest instant a wave of heat passed over her, spreading out all through her body. That same funny, silly, overwhelming sensation experienced by teenagers during the "did-he-notice-me-or-didn't-he?" ritual from years gone by.

Get a grip, Dee. You're not sixteen anymore.

She told herself she was just hallucinating, that what she felt was merely a by-product of countless nights with too little sleep because of the damned nightmares.

It had been years since she'd reacted to a man. Any man. And she intended to keep it that way.

"Then you'd be wasting your time," she told him softly.

Her voice, low, sexy and intoxicating, got under his skin. He was having some very unprofessional thoughts right now. "My time to waste."

She drew back, shifting gears. That had been a dangerous road she'd just touched on. Dangerous for her. "Not when the department is paying you. Daddy wouldn't like it."

She had the pleasure of watching the handsome detective stiffen. Obviously she'd stumbled across a button she could press if needed. She wondered if there was friction between the older and younger Cavanaughs.

The grin on Troy's lips hardened ever so slightly. "Are we going to play this game all evening or are you going to tell me what made you come back to the motel room where Petrie was killed? As far as I understand the duties of a probation officer, your business here is over."

He was putting her in her place. She didn't like that.

Delene took the upper hand. "Relax, Cavanaugh, this isn't an old-fashioned melodrama. The killer isn't coming back to the scene of the crime." Shoving her hands into her back pockets, she shifted slightly on the balls of her feet. It was a habit she had when she was searching for a way to calm down. "Clyde has a daughter."

"All right." Troy drew the words out, waiting for the woman to follow up the statement with more concrete information. "So he has a daughter. What's that got to do with you?"

Nothing. Everything. Because I was cursed with a conscience.

She ignored his question. "Her name was tattooed on his forearm."

He'd noticed the tattoo when he was examining the body. "Rachel" in common ink. "Not exactly top grade," he commented.

"He was probably stoned out of his mind when he got it. That doesn't promote the best judgment as to where to get one," she said. "He was lucky he didn't get blood poisoning from a dirty needle."

"Whatever luck he might have had ran out today," Troy said.

"Yeah, it did." She sighed, glancing around the room. Anywhere but at the chalked outline. "I figure his daughter has a right to know that he's dead and didn't just take off and leave her."

There was something in the way she said the last part that had him looking at Delene. And wondering.

"Is that the way it happened?" he asked softly. He

knew he was intruding, but she'd been the one who had inadvertently thrown it out there.

Delene pulled back her shoulders, as if unconsciously bracing for a blow. "What?"

"To you," he said, taking the same tone with her that his cousin Patience took with the wounded animals she cared for in her capacity as veterinarian. "Did your father leave your mother. And you?"

Her expression hardened. All traces of friendliness vanished. "Don't try to analyze me, Cavanaugh. You're out of your league. I just felt sorry for the poor slob. And for the little girl he brought into the world. End of story." All totaled, she'd worked with Clyde Petrie for almost three months, inheriting his file when another officer had retired. She'd made it a point to learn his background, to know what she was up against. "I know he tried to clean up twice, always saying that a daughter deserved to be proud of her father."

She looked around once more. The motel room looked no better in the late-afternoon light than it had in the predawn hours. An oppressive feeling of hopelessness seemed woven in with the stains and the grime. That and an almost disabling loneliness.

"I thought maybe he had her address here or a phone number." It was her intention to exhaust the regular avenues of search before resorting to the Internet.

Tying up those loose ends wasn't exactly within the probation department's jurisdiction, but he liked the way the woman thought. "Do you know what her mother's name is?" he asked.

Delene shook her head. "Clyde never married her so it's not on our records. I wouldn't have known about the girl at all except during one of the department's impromptu visits, I found Clyde sitting by the window, holding her picture. There were tears in his eyes. He told me she was four, maybe five. He wasn't too good with dates."

Troy had his own thoughts about the origin of those tears. Probably Clyde realized that he didn't have enough money to score, he thought. "Well, I guess he wasn't ready to take on the dad from *The Brady Bunch* for the title of Father of the Year."

She moved her shoulders in a half-dismissive shrug. "I suppose Clyde did the best he could, given how weak he was." This time she did look down at the chalk outline. "At least he tried."

What was she really doing here? Troy wondered. He caught himself wondering other things about her, as well. Things if he asked, he was confident he'd only get a flippant response to. He decided that once he was off-duty, he was going to do a little homework. See just what he could find out about Agent Delene D'Angelo. If all else failed, he was pretty sure he could always ask Brenda, his brother Dax's new wife. The woman could make a computer do anything but sit up and beg—and maybe even that, too.

"Want me to help you look around?" he offered.

The first response that occurred to Delene was she didn't want to be indebted to anyone. Favors required favors in return.

"It's not that big a place," she told him, then reconsidered. This was his crime scene, not hers. Technically he could order her off. "Sure, why not? Two sets of eyes are usually better than one." Approaching the largest pile of fast-food wrappers, discarded soda cups and stained carryout bags, she paused to take out her gloves. "What is it that *you're* looking for? Just in case I stumble across it first."

He gave her a grin that she found much too engaging. "I don't know."

Their eyes met. Hers were incredulous. "You don't know?"

Admitting it didn't seem to faze him, and she found that unusual. Most men liked to look as if they knew what they were doing.

"Nope. Just that I'll know it when I see it," he said.

Her mouth quirked and he felt something skip a beat inside his chest. Probably had to do with the burrito he'd had for breakfast. Ordinarily, three days out of five, breakfast time would find him at his uncle's house, seated at a table that never seemed to run out of leaves or chairs in its ever-expanding mode.

His father's older brother, Uncle Andrew, had put himself through the academy as a short-order cook in a diner. When he retired to raise what was, at the time, his motherless family, Uncle Andrew indulged himself in his only passion outside of law enforcement and his family. Cooking.

And when, one by one, the members of his family began to spread their wings and fly away from home, he'd insisted on having everyone return each morning for breakfast. To entice them, Andrew went all-out, preparing not just a meal but what could pass as a gourmet feast. Troy hadn't been able to make it to Uncle Andrew's house this morning, because of the homicide call. So breakfast had turned out to be the first semi-edible thing he could get his hands on.

Troy knew exactly what expression would descend over his uncle's face if the older man heard that he'd grabbed a breakfast burrito at a fast-food restaurant.

"You've obviously been watching too many cop shows," Delene was saying to him.

Actually, he found himself addicted to the slew of crime dramas that were on the air, taping the ones he didn't get a chance to watch. He flashed her another grin. "Doesn't make it any less true."

He thought he heard her say something about the level of intelligence of the new wave of detective these days, but he couldn't be sure. The next moment, she was riffling through the drawers in the battered and scarred bureau that dominated the wall beside the tiny bathroom.

He let the comment go.

Between them, they went over the entire length and breadth of the motel room, coming up empty when they finished.

It bothered Delene that she couldn't even find Rachel's photograph. She found it telling.

"Why is this significant?" Troy asked.

She closed the closet. The hangers had been empty.

Whatever clothing Clyde had possessed was in the heaps on the floor.

"Because someone must have taken the photo," she told him. "I know I saw it."

"Why would someone want to take a picture of a drug dealer's daughter? It's not as if they could kidnap her and hold her for ransom. It certainly doesn't look as if Clyde had any money."

"Not just any someone," she corrected him. "Her mother." Maybe the woman, whoever she was, didn't want him having anything to do with the little girl.

"Or," Troy theorized, "Petrie could have easily lost it."

Delene didn't believe that. She shook her head. "It meant too much to him."

"When he was sober," Troy pointed out. "All bets are off when he was high."

But Delene remained unmoved. "Some things remain constant, even for addicts."

He wondered if the woman even realized that she had become passionate about her subject. "Is that first-hand knowledge?" he asked.

Her chin rose defensively. "That's firsthand information. The people the county has on probation are not exactly all the crème de la crème."

Which led him to the question that had been echoing in his head since he first laid eyes on her this morning. He couldn't see her going down into the trenches, getting dirty in their filth. "What's a nice girl like you doing in a business like this?"

Now there was a line, Delene thought. "Earning a living."

"Got to be other ways to do it."

She looked at the piles of wrappers. It was hard not to just scoop them up and throw them away. She hated chaos, always had. "I like the hours," she quipped.

"You mean round-the-clock?" Troy scoffed. "What are you, a bat?"

"Get your facts straight, Detective. Bats don't operate during the day."

"Guess their union's stronger than yours." He finished going through the last pile and found that it was exactly what it appeared. Garbage. "Nothing," he announced, rising to his feet.

An exercise in futility. Delene bit back an oath. "Did you check out Mendoza yet?"

He'd placed a call to his sister to check out D'Angelo's story. When it rang true, he and Kara had gone to see the self-appointed drug lord at his opulent house, only to be told by one of Mendoza's underlings that the man was on vacation in Florida, visiting his sister. Troy didn't believe the excuse for a moment, but the location had a true ring to it.

"Mendoza's out of town."

She gave him a pointed look. "He wouldn't have to pull the trigger himself."

It was Troy's turn again to grin. "Trying to tell me how to do my job, D'Angelo?"

"Just making a helpful observation."

Before he could comment on the helpful nature of

her observations, a commotion outside the motel room had them both becoming alert. Troy had his weapon out in under a heartbeat.

"Stay here," he told her.

She had her own weapon and the department had spent its fair share of money training her on its use. She unholstered it.

"The hell I will," she declared, following him out.

Chapter 4

Troy bit off a curse. Why couldn't the woman stay in the room the way he told her to?

The next moment, the surge of adrenaline that began to sweep over him receded. There was no danger. At least, not the kind that left bullets in its wake. But something equally lethal had just made its appearance.

The local media.

Troy lowered his weapon and holstered it. A TV network news truck was parked over on the side and a perky strawberry-blonde with a microphone stood in the middle of the courtyard. The woman seemed undecided as to whether she wanted to flirt with the camera or come on as a seasoned professional, despite her very obvious pretty-doll appearance.

"Looks like a slow newsday at Channel Eight," he muttered more to himself than to the woman at his side.

The words were no sooner out than the reporter swung around and saw them. Recognizing authority, her expression lit up instantly.

There was no way he was going to hang around and be questioned, Troy thought. At least he'd had a chance to go through the dead man's room to his own satisfaction before the vultures descended.

"Time for me to go." He tossed the words toward Delene even as he headed for his rental car. Delene didn't answer, not that it surprised him. But she had fallen into step with him, keeping to his left side so that the motel was at her back. For all intents and purposes, his body hid her almost completely. If he didn't know any better, he would have said she was using him as a shield to block her from the reporter's view.

"You okay?" he asked.

"Keep walking," she ordered, her voice low, intense.

Delene had pulled her cap down to partially obscure her face, like a celebrity in hiding. It was obvious that she definitely didn't want the eye of the camera to find her.

What gives? he wondered.

He didn't have time to speculate or wait for an answer. The reporter with her cameraman had descended on them. He never slowed his pace but kept walking toward his vehicle as if the woman wasn't pushing a microphone toward his face.

Undaunted, the woman pressed on. "Detective, what can you tell us about what happened here?"

Never breaking stride, Troy gave the woman his most charming smile, gambling that it would deflect any attention the reporter might have been inclined to give Delene. "You know that we can't talk about an ongoing investigation, even if we wanted to."

For a second, the woman seemed physically touched by his smile. She beamed at him in response, attempting a little charm of her own.

"Oh, c'mon, Detective. It'll be in all the papers by morning. Why not give me a break?" Tossing her hair over her shoulder as she nodded toward the motel room with its harsh yellow tape that proclaimed it a crime scene. "Wasn't the victim supposed to testify against Miguel Mendoza in next month's trial?"

He traded his charming expression for one of pure innocence. "Looks like you know more than me, ma'am," he told her just as he reached his car.

Unlocking the driver's side, he glanced up to see that instead of continuing on to her car, Delene had thrown herself into the passenger seat of his. She tugged her cap down even lower until the brim was touching her nose.

Not exactly the last word in subtle, he thought, getting in himself.

"Agent D'Angelo, this is so sudden," he cracked. "Your place or mine?"

After inserting his key in the ignition, Troy turned on the engine. The vehicle made a few strange noises, testifying that as a rental it hadn't received the best of treatment. He hoped it would last until he got his own car back.

"Drive." The order emerged from beneath the khaki cap.

"Yes, ma'am." Once he backed up, Troy turned the car around and pulled out of the lot. Glancing back, he saw that the cameraman was still filming. A *really* slow news day. He looked over at the passenger seat where Delene was slouched down. "You can come up for air now."

She sat up, pulling the cap off her head. Delene dragged her fingers through her hair, taking away its flatness before leaning forward to stuff her cap into her back pocket.

Troy waited to be enlightened, but in vain. "Mind telling me what that was all about?"

Delene kept her face forward, staring straight ahead as dusk softly embraced the city streets. She let out the breath she'd been holding. That could have been disastrous, she thought.

"I don't like reporters."

No one in his family had a soft spot in their hearts for the people who made their livelihood on tragedy and disaster. "Neither do I, but I don't fold up like a piece of origami paper when one of them approaches me with a microphone."

She shrugged. Her bangs fell into her eyes and she combed them back with her fingers. He caught a whiff of something soft and herbal. Clean. Probably her shampoo.

"We all do things our own way." Delene didn't follow up the flippant answer by saying that she had a fear of having her picture taken or being captured on film. That she was afraid that maybe, just maybe, Russell would see the end result and realize where she was. That he'd come looking for her.

His seeing the film clip was, of course, only a remote possibility, but she'd gone through too much to get careless now. The consequences were too huge. If she had a choice between being supercautious or supersorry, she'd pick cautious every time.

They drove down another street. Delene hadn't ventured a single extra word. "Any particular place you'd like me to drive to?"

She shrugged again, as if he should already know the answer. Her agitation level had definitely gone up, he noted. What had he missed? Did she know that reporter? Or the cameraman? And why had she hidden her face like that? He didn't know her, but she didn't strike him as the type to hide from anyone.

"Just around until that news truck leaves and I can go back to my car."

"Right."

On the following block, they passed several restaurants, all in a fashionable row. Italian cuisine, a steakhouse and a quaint restaurant that could have doubled as the cottage where the Seven Dwarfs lived. There was smoke coming from the chimney. He glanced toward Delene. Since she obviously wanted to kill some time, they might as well make it pleasant.

"Buy you a cup of coffee, Agent D'Angelo?"

"Hmm?" She looked at him as if that would help her replay his question in her head. It obviously did because she said, "No, thanks."

Coffee was the main ingredient that kept him and his family going, but he supposed there were those who didn't care for the brew. "Tea?"

She shook her head, her face averted as she glanced out the front windshield. "No."

Undaunted, he tried again. "Soda? A drink? A cup of air?" he finally asked when she didn't respond to the first two choices.

Her expression was impassive. "I don't drink."

"But you do breathe."

A hint of a smile flirted with one of the corners of her mouth. "On occasion."

What did it take to make her smile? he wondered. Really smile? He felt a challenge coming on. One that he was up to.

The light up ahead turned red. He eased down on the brake, his headlights casting beams on the back of the black SUV he was behind.

"What about the drinking?" he asked. "Is that a religious thing or just a personal preference?"

This had been a mistake. She should have sprinted toward her own car instead of getting into his, Delene upbraided herself—even if that would have left her exposed for a few moments. At least she would have already been on her way home by now instead of being subjected to this cross-examination.

She could feel his eyes on her, even though he had started driving again. "Not that it's any business of yours, but it's personal."

Troy waited a beat. "How personal?"

Eyes that could have frozen a fire in midflash turned toward him. "*Very* personal."

Her manner only served to intrigue him. "Someone in your family drink too much?"

The man was more intuitive than she'd first thought. And this made her uneasy.

To her further surprise, she heard herself giving a tentative answer. "Maybe."

"Your mother?"

Her uneasiness grew. How could he know that? Heartbroken, not wanting to burden her daughter with her worries and insecurities, her mother had sought the kind of comfort that poured out two fingers' worth at a time. And thus only succeeded in worrying her more.

Doing her best to keep her thoughts from her face, Delene asked, "Why would you guess my mother instead of my father?" To her, that would have been the logical assumption.

They drove by a mall that boasted fifteen different theaters. The marquee was just lighting up. "Because he left you."

"I never said that," she pointed out quickly. She didn't want this man poking around in her life. "You just assumed it."

"But I was right, wasn't I?"

Delene fell silent. She supposed that it did no harm to admit this tiny part. After all, it didn't illuminate who she was, wouldn't send him off on any trails toward the truth. It was just an isolated fact.

One that saddened her whenever she let herself think about it.

"Yes."

He glanced at her, trying to gauge her tone. "On both counts?"

Delene blew out a breath. "You just don't stop, do you?"

Actually, Troy thought of his relentlessness as an asset, considering his line of work. His cousin Callie said he was like a bloodhound on the trail of a scent that was fifteen days old. He just didn't give up until he got what he was after.

He flashed Delene a grin. "There were eleven of us when I was growing up. You stopped, you got run over. Or missed out." Shy and retiring just didn't work in his family.

Delene's eyes widened in disbelief. She'd thought that Jorge and Adrian had been exaggerating earlier. They were prone to that.

"Eleven children?" she echoed. He had to be pulling her leg. Nobody had big families anymore. Three was considered large by today's standards. "Your mother had eleven children?" she repeated, waiting for him to own up to the exaggeration.

"No," he laughed. "My mother had four kids. But I

have seven cousins. There's maybe ten years' difference between the oldest to the youngest. And we were all very close, even when we were fighting. Especially when we were fighting," he corrected, remembering some of the finer exchanges of blows that had taken place. But the only casualties that resulted were skinned knees and knuckles, not feelings.

At least in the very beginning, he added silently. That was before Uncle Mike had allowed his jealousy of his brothers to drive them apart. He and his family still turned up at some of the functions, but there was a difference, a sadness that emanated from Patience and Patrick that even he could feel. None of the younger Cavanaughs had realized just how deeply the wounds ran until Uncle Mike had been killed in the line of duty. After that, certain facts slowly made their way to the surface.

His late uncle never felt he measured up to either his younger or especially his older brother. It turned him bitter. While he was still a decent cop, he wasn't as good as Andrew or Brian. He took his feelings of inadequacy out on his family. And looked elsewhere for gratification. When he turned to Uncle Andrew's wife, Rose, it resulted in near tragedy.

Not knowing what to think, what to believe, Uncle Andrew had argued with Aunt Rose. She left the house in a huff and disappeared for fifteen years. Everyone thought she was dead until Uncle Andrew, who had never given up hope, had finally managed to locate her. Aunt Rose had been in a car accident the morning she left. The head injury she'd suffered, along with the emotional strain she was under, caused her to forget who she was. It had taken love and patience, not to mention an incredible amount of luck, something he'd always believed in, to bring Aunt Rose back to herself.

But that was a story he figured he could tell Delene once he found out hers.

If he found out hers, he amended.

"You were lucky." The words were uttered so softly, had the radio been on, he wouldn't have heard them.

But he had. And he'd also heard her tone, pregnant with unspoken angst. "And you weren't."

Delene sighed, shifting in her seat. He was cornering her. She hated feeling cornered. Russell would always corner her. Physically and emotionally. Chipping away at her until she caved.

But that was then, this was now. And she didn't cave anymore. Or answer questions she didn't want to answer.

"You really don't stop, do you?" She glanced at the clock on the dashboard. They'd been driving for fifteen minutes. The fluffy reporter should have been all talked out by now. "I think it's safe for you to take me back now, Detective Cavanaugh."

"Whatever you say."

Shifting over to the extreme left lane, Troy made a U-turn at the next light and went back the way he'd come. Several minutes went by. Silence filled the spacious vehicle, and he knew if he didn't say anything, neither would she. It wasn't a silence he felt comfortable with. They didn't know each other well enough for that.

Finally he said, "Back there at the motel, when I told you to stay inside the room, you came out anyway without knowing who could have been outside. It might have been the killer coming back to make sure Petrie was dead." He spared her a glance. "You don't take orders very well, do you?"

Delene looked at him sharply. She didn't like being told what to do. Her days of being meek and subservient were long gone. "I don't take orders at all."

Troy slowed down, allowing a grocery delivery truck to pass him. "That must make it tough for your boss."

"I follow procedures, Cavanaugh. I stick to the guidelines," she informed him crisply. "But I don't like being bossed around by someone who thinks he's got the right to take the lead just because he can go to the bathroom standing up."

Blowing out a breath, but not her agitation, Delene turned her face forward. A fine mist of rain began to layer itself on the windshield. She hated rain—had hated it ever since she was a little girl. It made her feel lonely.

It had rained the night she'd made good her escape.

"Stop trying to pigeonhole me," she added as a warning.

That was a laugh, he thought. If ever there was a woman who didn't fit into a neat little niche, it was her. "Wouldn't dream of it. Just trying to get a feel for the woman."

She'd be willing to bet that as far as "feeling women" went, Detective Troy Cavanaugh had done far more than his fair share. Most likely, with that sexy grin of his and good looks, he had women lined up in droves. But she wasn't interested.

"Stop trying to do that, too."

One minute, she came on like gangbusters, the next she was withdrawing like a sunflower at dusk. What was she hiding? "Not exactly the talkative type, are you?"

Give the man a cigar, she thought sarcastically. "If by that you mean do I feel the need to spill my insides to every stranger I meet? I don't."

"We've stood over a dead body together, we're hardly strangers."

She glared at him, wondering what it would take to make the man back off. Why was he so intent on getting her to talk? What was his angle? "And we're hardly bosom buddies, either."

The grin he flashed at her was positively wicked. "There's a remedy for that."

The frost was back in her eyes. "Do women usually find this line of conversation charming?" Her question was downright insulting, but she felt it might be the only way she could get him to back off.

From the look on his face, she'd failed. Was he too thick to realize she'd just put him down?

"I don't know. I've never taken a poll. But most people like me."

She snorted. "Then you'll be able to find yourself a playmate once I'm out of your car."

He paused for a long moment and she thought she'd finally gotten him to shut up. Her triumph was very short-lived. "Why are you trying so hard to seem tough, Agent D'Angelo?"

Because it's the only way I can survive. "Maybe there's no 'seem' about it," she shot back. "Maybe I am tough."

"'Tough' doesn't come back to rummage through a dead junkie's things looking for his daughter's address so she can break the news to her personally."

Why didn't he leave her alone? She certainly wasn't in the market to get hit on. Men weren't worth the trouble. If he'd done nothing else, Russell had taught her that. "I'm not interested in your theories, Cavanaugh."

His voice was light, as if they were sharing a friendly conversation. Maybe the man was dense, she decided.

"Too bad," he said. "Because I'm interested in anything you have to say." They were back at the motel again. Most of the parking spaces were filled, but the news truck was nowhere to be seen. He guided the Lincoln Continental into the first available spot he could find. After cutting the engine, he shifted to look at her. "That offer for coffee still stands."

"And it'll have to continue to stand." She wrapped her fingers around the door handle and pushed. Nothing happened. She tried again with the same results. She eyed him expectantly. "Okay, how do I get out of here?"

Rather than try to explain, he showed her. His body

was all but touching hers as he reached over to the handle, creating a very cozy, intimate space. Their eyes met and he had to restrain a very strong urge to kiss this woman who seemed so intent on giving him a hard time.

"It's tricky." His breath slid over her face as the words emerged. "You have to jiggle it."

"Oh." Her heart hammered, making the pulse in her throat vibrate in time. "You didn't have to give me a demonstration. Just telling me would have been enough."

"I'm a hands-on kind of guy." The words were soft, teasing. His breath was irresistible.

The moment stood still. Held in abeyance. Waiting.

"I'll just bet you are," she finally said, forcing herself to pull back instead of lean forward, the way she wanted to. *Run!* a voice in her head ordered.

"Need an escort home?" he asked just as she was about to exit.

Delene looked at him. Something shimmied down her spine even as suspicion danced over her. This was getting to be downright creepy. Was Cavanaugh just incredibly intuitive, or was there another reason why his random guesses were so on the mark? Could he somehow be working for Russell? Like the detective, Russell was not without his charm. It emanated from his every pore, and until he acted otherwise, displaying his true nature, his charm seemed genuine enough.

No, she was letting her imagination run away with her. There was no earthly reason for Cavanaugh to be connected to Russell. The Cavanaughs had a dynasty. They stood for the law. Russell stood for the exact opposite. Had made his fortune that way.

Still, she couldn't loosen the grip that tension had over her. "What makes you say that?"

"The cap thing," he reminded her. "I've only seen celebrities and people with something to hide behave that way." When she said nothing, he went on. "If you are hiding from someone or something—"

She wasn't going to have him go that route. She didn't want him stumbling across the truth. "Standing beside a seven-foot—"

"Six-three," he corrected. "I'm six foot three."

She waved a dismissive hand in the air. "Whatever. Standing next to a giant is not the way to keep a low profile."

He gleaned what he needed from her words. "Then you are hiding from someone?"

"Just going along with your analogy, nothing more," she told him, impatient. This time, she threw open the door and got out. "Thanks for the ride, Detective."

He ducked his head down a little so he could continue to see her as she made her way to her own vehicle. "Don't mention it. Any time you want to ride around in circles, just give me a call."

Getting into her own car, Delene shook her head and closed the door. Cavanaugh was amusing as well as drop-dead good-looking. But she wanted neither to be amused, nor to drop dead. Especially the latter.

The only thing she was in the market for was surviving. If she managed that, everything else was just a bonus.

After locking the doors and buckling up, Delene put the key into the ignition, turning on her engine and headlights. Looking over her shoulder, she pulled out of the spot and then out of the parking lot.

The moment she was out on the street, Troy followed her.

Chapter 5

Delene glanced into her rearview mirror a second before she made the right-hand turn. The car was still there, one length behind.

Okay, what the hell was he trying to prove?

Because she rarely relaxed and because Clyde's death had elevated her stress level, Delene was even more alert than usual. Which meant she'd spotted the other vehicle instantly. It was no coincidence. The car had been behind her the entire trip from the seedy Traveler's Motel parking lot and was now entering the apartment complex a minute after she'd made the turn.

Delene pulled her worn Toyota into its carport space. Turning off the engine, and with it the almost muted strains of the radio station, she sat behind the wheel and waited to see what the driver of the car that had been tailing her would do next.

Rather than drive on, he came to a stop in one of the extra parking spaces across the way.

For a second, Delene toyed with the idea of pulling out again, of leading the car on a convoluted chase down back alleys and dark streets before losing him. She knew she was more than capable of doing just that after taking a course in evasive driving from a school that specialized in training the chauffeurs of high-profile executives as well as of the rich and famous.

But what would be the point of that? He only had to come back here to find her. And besides, she knew who was behind the wheel.

What she didn't know was why.

But she intended to find out.

Now.

Delene got out of the car and locked it before marching over to the parked Lincoln Continental. And Troy Cavanaugh.

The detective rolled down the window as she approached. He didn't even have the decency to look chagrined at being caught.

"You're parked there illegally, you know." Unlike her space, which was marked Reserved, Cavanaugh had brought his car to a stop in one marked Permit Parking.

He seemed unfazed by the information. "I wasn't planning on staying long."

"Why were you planning on staying at all?" she asked. She lowered her face to his level. The window was at half-mast. There was nothing between them but strangely warm air. "Are you stalking me, Detective Cavanaugh?"

Her expression was unreadable. A woman like this would have been a perfect model for a sphinx. Even under scrutiny, he couldn't be sure if she was being serious or not. Most people didn't think of stalkers right off the bat. Her question, flippant or otherwise, made him wonder if she'd encountered a stalker in her time. That would go a long way toward explaining things.

Such disturbing incidents were far more common than most people cared to admit. In his own family, despite the preponderance of law-enforcement agents, his cousin Patience had had not just one stalker, but two. What made things worse was that the second one had been an officer on the Aurora police force.

You just never knew. Stalkers came in all sizes, shapes and walks of life.

"Watching over you," he told her, allowing just a shade of the annoyance he felt get through.

"And just what makes you think that I need watching over?"

He wouldn't want to be caught on the other side of her anger when it finally hit its high point. "Just a hunch."

"Sorry to disappoint you, but your hunch is wrong, Cavanaugh."

He shrugged nonchalantly, as if it was all one and the same to him. "Been known to happen before," he allowed. "But not with any kind of frequency you could chart."

She could feel his eyes washing over her. Taking stock. She didn't like being analyzed or measured.

"There anything you want to talk about?" he asked.

She returned his gaze without flinching. If he wanted to play the staring game, he'd picked the wrong person to pit himself against. "Other than the detective who won't go home? No."

The old saying about leading a horse to water drifted through his head. He certainly couldn't force her to talk to him, even though he was pretty certain there *was* something she needed to get off her chest.

Other than the obvious, he couldn't help thinking. But that was the unattached bachelor in him, the one who enjoyed the company of beautiful women, no strings attached.

He had a feeling she wouldn't appreciate knowing his thoughts right now. He took out one of his cards from his jacket pocket and held it out to her. "You can reach me at this number if you change your mind."

She made no move to take it. Instead, she looked at the card as if it would permanently stain her fingers if she touched it. "I won't."

He continued to hold it out for her. "Humor me."

She laughed dryly. "I bet you say that to all the girls."

So she did have a sense of humor. "Only the stubborn ones," he told her.

Delene frowned. She had a feeling that Cavanaugh

was going to sit out here all night if she didn't take the damn card.

"If it'll make you go away," she muttered.

As she tucked his card into her pocket, Delene glanced up toward her apartment. It was a purely reflexive action, like glancing at her watch when she already knew the time.

When she'd first moved to Aurora, she'd deliberately rented an apartment on the third floor, one without a fire escape so that there was only one way in, one way out. Her other specification was that the living quarters be a loft. That way she had a sweeping view of the entire apartment the moment she walked into it.

Looking up at the window that faced the carport, she froze. The apartment looked completely dark.

"Something wrong?" It was a rhetorical question. He knew there had to be. No one looked like that if everything was all right.

"The light's not on." The words came out before she realized she'd spoken them.

He interpreted the only way he could. "You live with someone?"

"No." She continued to stare at the darkened window. Her voice was deadly quiet. "But I always leave one light on when I leave the apartment."

It seemed to him a waste of electricity, but this wasn't the time to debate that. If she'd left the light on and it was off, that meant someone had turned it off. Getting out of the rented vehicle, Troy glanced up at the apartment in question and saw that the window gave no hint of illumination within.

He held out his hand. "Give me your keys. I'll check it out."

The suggestion that she wasn't capable of doing that on her own had her on the defensive. "I don't need a bodyguard."

What was this woman's problem? He was only trying to be helpful. "Look, you're obviously afraid of something—"

Her eyes narrowed. She couldn't even bring herself to entertain that thought. Because if she did, it would become a reality. "I am not afraid—"

"Okay, call it whatever you want to call it. I don't have a thesaurus at my disposal at the moment. But it's damn obvious from where I'm standing that you're not exactly overjoyed about the situation." Annoyed, Troy thrust his hand out again. "Now give me your damn keys and let me go up."

She supposed it wouldn't hurt to have a little muscle backing her up. But she wasn't about to let him get the upper hand. No man was going to occupy that position with her again.

"We'll do it together."

He would have been happier if she stayed in his car. Taking the key she reluctantly handed over, he turned toward the cluster of six garden apartments where her unit was located.

"You have got to be the most stubborn woman I've ever met—and considering the women in my family, that's saying a hell of a lot." Troy deliberately got in front of her when they reached the stone steps that led to the first landing.

"Flattery will get you nowhere," she bit off.

Troy paused to look back at her a second before going on to the second flight of stairs. "That wasn't meant as a compliment."

It was to her. Stubbornness had been the key component to her survival. If she hadn't been stubborn, she wouldn't have been able to cling to life in that hospital bed. There was no doubt in her mind that she would have died there, on the fifth floor of Mercy General. It was stubbornness that had given her the will to live when another woman in her place would have felt she had nothing to live for. And it was stubbornness that had her utilizing the opportunity she'd inadvertently been given to make good her escape from a life that had promised her demise.

Coming to the third-floor landing, several steps before her door, Troy took out his gun before inserting Delene's key into the lock. He turned it very slowly, then pushed open the door.

Nothing happened. The interior was pitch black.

From behind him, a small, high-powered beam of light cut into the darkness. When he looked, he saw that Delene was shining a flashlight into her apartment.

The woman was nothing if not prepared, he thought. He hadn't even seen it in her possession. Silently he extended his hand. She placed the flashlight into it.

Troy crossed the threshold and swept over the entrance with the flashlight. Very carefully he extended the arc he created until every shadow had danced with the light beam, leaving no corner untouched.

There was no one in the loft.

The next moment, the apartment was bathed in artificial light. Delene had turned on the main switch located just beside the doorjamb. No longer standing behind him but beside him, Delene quickly looked around.

Nothing appeared to have been disturbed. And yet, she didn't relax.

Had whoever had come in just taken in the lay of the land and then left? Or was he hiding in the walk-in closet? she thought suddenly.

As if reading her mind, Troy crossed to the loft's single closet. Pausing for the count of two, he then jerked open the door. The closet wasn't overly large but seemed that much bigger because there was so little in it.

His sister with her high-powered suits could take a lesson from this woman, Troy thought. He wondered if Delene subscribed to the "less is more" theory. Her paychecks certainly weren't finding their way to the local department stores. But he had a feeling she would have looked good even dressed in colored construction paper.

He turned away from the closet and followed the same procedure with the bathroom. With the same results.

"Nothing." A look tinged in skepticism came into

his eyes. She was human and humans were sometimes forgetful. "Are you sure you turned on the light before you left?"

"I'm sure," she snapped, then regretted being so short-tempered. After all, he didn't have to go out of his way like this. But then, she hadn't asked him to in the first place. She owed the man nothing, not even polite answers. "I *always* turn it on."

"Seems like a waste of electricity to me."

"Peace of mind, priceless," Delene countered, paraphrasing a famous credit card commercial.

Because being so close to him made her feel antsy, she walked over to the floor lamp and reached beneath the pleated shade to switch it on. Nothing happened. She tried twice more with the same results.

"Looks like it blew out," Troy observed, coming over to the lamp.

When he tilted it so that he could look down at the top, he saw a deep black spot in the center of the bulb. At the same time, he glanced at the digital clock radio on the kitchen counter. The bright blue numbers that recorded the time were flashing, the way they would have had the unit just been plugged in and not set. The clock was flashing 4:20.

He came to the obvious conclusion. "I think there was a power outage around here," he guessed. "Approximately four hours ago." Though she tried to mask it, he heard the sigh of relief as it escaped her lips. "Why do you leave your light on when you go out?"

Her excuse was automatic. "I don't like coming home to a dark apartment."

"That the only reason?"

She lifted her chin. Definitely reminded him of his girl cousins, he thought. Both Teri and Rayne had the same habit. It was as if they were daring him to take a swing, safe in the knowledge that he wouldn't.

"I could make something up for you if you'd like," she retorted.

He had a feeling that she already had. "Want me to stick around for a few minutes while you look under the bed and get your bearings?"

He was mocking her. She hated being the butt of a joke. Hated it with a passion. Because she had been. She'd been the butt of Russell's vicious jokes.

"No." Her tone was dismissive. "All I want right now is to take a hot bath and relax."

It was easier than he thought possible for him to envision that. To see her shedding her unflattering uniform and slipping into filmy suds. The excellent figure D'Angelo possessed was not completely hidden by her uniform. There was enough of a hint for his healthy imagination to be off and running.

"Maybe I want to stick around," he told her.

He thought he saw the faintest glimmer of a smile cross her lips. "Sorry. The house makes the rules and this is my house. You leave." She nodded toward the door. And then she dropped her flippant tone for a moment. "And thanks."

Troy hadn't expected her to say that. The woman

had just spent the past ten minutes fighting his presence, tooth and nail.

"No need to thank me, D'Angelo." His smile was warm, easy and slipped over her like a soft evening wrap. "It's my job. Serve and protect, right?"

Delene realized that she hadn't drawn a breath. She took one before answering. A long one. "Right."

At the door, he turned around to look at her again. She'd followed him and had to step back to avoid a collision. As it was, he brushed against her. And felt some kind of static-laced response. But the air was moist, not dry. Static electricity only made an appearance when it was dry, he thought.

So why...?

She'd felt it, too, he realized, looking into her face. He stopped questioning the phenomenon and just enjoyed it. Troy nodded toward her breast pocket, where she'd placed the card he'd given her.

"Keep that card handy."

She had to stop herself from touching it. She told herself it made no difference to her if the card was still in her pocket or not. There was no reason to see if it was. "I won't be needing to call you."

He merely grinned. "You never know when another bulb might blow out."

The second Troy stepped over her threshold, she closed the door behind him. He heard her throw the lock, then slip a chain into place, barring any access— at least to weaklings. A burly man could probably put his shoulder into it and rip that sucker out.

A man like that Jorge character who'd been with her this morning, he recalled. Not a bad man to use as a bodyguard, either. He wondered why she hadn't sought his help with this "thing," whatever it was.

The woman was definitely afraid of something. Troy was thoughtful as he went back to his vehicle. Anyone with eyes could see her fear, despite how hard she attempted to cover it.

He wondered where this need to be superhuman had come from.

Had someone threatened her? It took no stretch of the imagination to believe that. Delene undoubtedly dealt with unsavory types all the time. You didn't exactly meet the best class of people as a probation officer.

Had she stepped on someone's toes? Rated someone's displeasure? Incurred someone's anger? Miguel Mendoza and his little so-called cartel wasn't exactly small potatoes. Was he the one after her for some reason?

Or was something else going on? He recalled the look on her face when she stared up at her apartment window. There'd been vulnerability there, just for a split second.

He wanted to find out why.

After being with the police department for several years, he'd built up more than a few sources. Not to mention that he could fall back on the combined resources of his law-enforcement family.

He got into his roomy vehicle and turned the engine

and headlights back on. When he'd fired up his ignition, the oldies station came on the radio. The interior of the vehicle was the site of another British invasion as the musical group The Animals lamented the possibility of being misunderstood.

He figured it should be an easy enough matter to find out if there was some kind of contract out on the street with Delene D'Angelo's name on it.

He couldn't see her being afraid of anything else. She wasn't the type.

But in the meantime, he reminded himself as he shifted into Reverse and crept out of the spot, he had a case to solve.

Standing at her window, Delene watched as Troy pulled the oversize boat of a car out of its spot and onto the street. She stood there a long moment, her gaze sweeping over the parking lot—just in case—before letting the curtain fall back into place.

She had to get a grip on herself. If she didn't, then her escape would have been for nothing. And if she didn't, it was only a matter of time before her boss would notice and make a recommendation that she visit the department shrink. That was the last thing she wanted to do. Talking to someone about her fears wasn't going to help, wasn't going to make them go away. Or make them any less real to her.

This was something she had to tackle on her own. And she would. Just like she'd conquered everything else herself. She knew that while she worked with people who were friendly enough, whom she even liked, there was really no one in her corner but her. It was one of life's harsh realities that she'd learned before she'd ever become Delene D'Angelo.

You couldn't rely on anyone but yourself.

You couldn't even rely on your own mother. That, too, she'd learned before she'd ever stepped foot in Aurora. She'd made one attempt at escape before she'd succeeded. She'd gone back home, to her mother, begging the woman to hide her for a little while. Her mother had recently moved to another city and Delene was certain that Russell didn't know the new address.

He didn't have to. Her mother had called him shortly after she'd made her appearance. Called him and told him that she was hiding there. Russell came to get her in the middle of the night. He'd been all charm and smiles for her mother's benefit, slipping her several folded hundred-dollar bills just before he'd taken her daughter's arm and led her out the door to his waiting limousine.

It wasn't until they were inside the sleek black vehicle, with its soundproof glass separating them from the stone-faced driver, that Russell had taken out his rage on her. Beating her with his fists. Careful to leave bruises only where no one else could ever see them.

She supposed she'd been lucky that he had completely lost his temper that last time. If he hadn't, if he hadn't gone berserk and beaten her within an inch of her life, she never would have been taken to the hospital.

Never escaped.

She hoped that Russell never found out about the orderly who'd helped her. When she could bring herself to pray, she prayed for the young man's safety.

She walked over to her computer and switched it on. A soft hum filled the silence as it went through its paces. She'd lied to Cavanaugh. She had no intentions of taking a bubble bath. Luxuries like that were beyond her ability to enjoy. She couldn't relax in a tub. Stripped naked and reposing in sudsy water just made her feel vulnerable. It was hard enough shutting her eyes each night and trying to sleep.

What she had planned for tonight was doing what she could to try to track down Clyde's daughter. The girl deserved closure. It was the least she could do for Clyde, Delene thought. Seeing as how she was the one who had talked the man into giving evidence against Mendoza in the first place.

After taking a can of diet soda from the refrigerator, Delene sat down at the table. Her fingers flew over several keys, as she connected to the Internet. A thought that had been nagging at her since she'd returned to the motel room moved forward in her brain.

What if it wasn't Mendoza, or more accurately, one of his men, who had killed Clyde? But if not Mendoza, then who? A disgruntled junkie? Someone wanting Clyde's stash? They hadn't found any drugs or money in the room, so it could have been something as simple as a robbery gone wrong.

Except that they didn't know if there were any drugs

or money to be gotten. Most of the time, Clyde was completely tapped out.

Delene sighed. She had an entire boatload of cases on her desk back at the probation office, demanding her attention. Just like everyone else. They were all overloaded at the department. She had no excuse for devoting any more time to a case where the man whose name was on the top of the file was dead.

No excuse but her own conscience.

It was enough.

As the musical tones of her service provider came on, cheerfully welcoming her back, Delene began to type.

Chapter 6

"I've got good news and I've got bad news," Eric Blalock, the crime scene investigation's technician from Ballistics, said to Troy as he approached his desk. The gangly blond's lopsided grin dared him to go for the bad first. "What order do you want to hear it in?"

Troy looked up from the latest notes he'd just been handed. It had been three days since Delene and company had discovered Petrie's body and called in the homicide. All three of their statements had already been taken and processed. So far, they were going nowhere in the investigation, despite the man hours he and Kara had put in.

He pushed back from his desk. "I could use a little good news, Eric. Hit me with that first."

Eric took a deep breath and launched into his presentation. "As you know, the bullet responsible for taking Clyde Petrie's life was in almost perfect condition."

Troy spun his hand around rapidly, signaling that the technician should speed it up. Eric had a tendency to be long-winded once he got going. "Give me the short version, Eric."

Looking somewhat petulant at having to abbreviate his moment of glory, Eric nevertheless did as he was asked. "The gun's been used before. Specifically in the commission of a bank robbery. One of the bullets found its way into the leg of a sixty-seven-year-old security guard."

This gave them someone to look at, Troy thought, heartened. "And the bad news?"

Eric placed his report on Troy's desk. "Joe Sheffield, the guy whose gun it was, is still in prison, so he can't be your guy."

"Wait a minute." Drawn by the technician's voice, Kara came around the side of the cubicle to join the two men. "If they got the bank robber, shouldn't his weapon be in the property room?"

Eric looked a tad sheepish. "That's actually worse news."

"You didn't say there was 'worse news,'" Troy pointed out as he leaned forward in his chair.

"I didn't want to bum you out right away," Eric confessed. "The gun was never found. They convicted him anyway because his mask slipped as he was running off with the money and they got it on the surveillance tape."

"Best-laid plans of mice and men," Troy murmured under his breath. He wished all the criminals they came across were as inept as the former owner of the gun.

Kara looked at Troy. "Maybe Sheffield gave someone the gun for 'safekeeping.'"

"If he had any brains, he would have thrown the gun away." Troy got to his feet. A long shot was better than no shot at all. "C'mon, Kara. Let's go pay the man a visit anyway."

Wearing the baggy orange jumpsuit that served as the county's prison garb, Joe Sheffield sat with his feet sprawled out before him as he indolently eyed his two unexpected visitors. His contempt for the duo and law-enforcement agents in general fairly reeked from every pore of his wide body.

"Dunno what gun you're talking about. I never robbed no bank. I'm a victim of mistaken identity," he maintained when Troy asked him for the second time what had happened to the gun he'd used when he'd tried to rob the bank.

"We're not here to debate your innocence or guilt, Sheffield," Troy said evenly.

"Then you're wasting my time," Sheffield informed them.

"Your gun was used in a homicide," Kara said.

Sheffield's expression never changed. He crossed his arms defiantly before him, staring straight at the female member of the duo in the room. "Couldn't have been. I don't own a gun. Never did."

"C'mon, Kara, we're wasting our time with Johnny One-Note here." Troy rose from the table, his eyes steely as he eyed the prisoner. "I don't know what you're looking to gain by this."

A bloodless smile curved the full lips. "Nothin'. I just like watching you people squirm."

Troy paused at the doorway, allowing Kara to cross the threshold first. A guard was already rousting the manacled Sheffield to his feet. "From where I stand, you're the one squirming, Sheffield. And it's going to be for a really long time."

Sheffield's smile vanished and he shouted an obscenity after Troy.

"Well, that went real well," Kara commented as they walked out.

"Wait," Troy cautioned, an optimistic note in his voice. "It's not over yet." He had a feeling that Sheffield would change his mind about talking once he had an opportunity to mull the situation over. The man didn't strike him as the sharpest knife in the drawer, but neither was he the dullest.

Troy and Kara had just enough time to return to the station and reach their respective desks before the phone call came in.

It was Sheffield's lawyer. The man went straight to the point. "My client says he might have something to tell you if you can offer him something."

Troy gave his partner the high-five sign. "Such as?"

The lawyer paused. "He wants a transfer to Folsom," he said, citing the more progressive prison. "He misses working out."

Just what the world needed, Troy thought. A stronger convict. But if it gave them what they wanted, that was how they were going to have to play it.

"Depends on what he has to give us." Troy's tone indicated that there would be no problem with the transfer.

"Understood."

"We'll be there within the hour." Troy ended the conversation just as Kara approached him. "We're hitting the road again."

Kara sighed, making a U-turn to retrieve the all-weather coat she'd just shed. "Mother warned me there'd be days like this."

They were back in the small room, facing Sheffield forty-five minutes later. The man's cocky attitude was replaced by one of compliance, due, Troy judged, in no small part to the conservatively dressed, silver-haired man at his elbow. Sheffield's lawyer.

His unmanacled hands folded before him as if he were a schoolboy sitting before the principal, Sheffield surrendered his bargaining chip. "I sold the gun."

"You sold it," Troy repeated, not quite certain if he believed the convict or if he was being set up for something. He glanced toward the lawyer, who wore an impassive expression. Troy decided he wouldn't have wanted to play poker with the older man. His eyes were unreadable. Just like his sister Janelle's were when she was in a game.

"Yeah, just before I got arrested," Sheffield said. Then, because he had nothing to lose and because he wanted to seem honest, he added, "Figured it was hot."

Troy's eyes never left Sheffield's face. The convict was easier to read than his lawyer. "Most people would have thrown it in the lake."

Sheffield looked contemptuous of the suggestion. "Hey, it set me back three bills. I wasn't going to just throw that away."

Troy glanced at the lawyer's face. The man was shaking his head, obviously incredulous at what he'd just heard. Troy suppressed a grin. The workings of the criminal mind never ceased to amaze him. "Okay, who'd you sell it to?"

Sheffield lifted his wide shoulders in a dismissive shrug. "My dealer."

Bells went off in his head. Troy exchanged glances with Kara. "Your dealer's name wouldn't happen to have been Clyde Petrie, would it?"

Sheffield's dark eyebrows drew together, knotting over the bridge of his hook nose like an oversize black caterpillar. He stared at Troy, clearly mystified. "Yeah, how d'you know that?"

"Because that's the man whose homicide we're investigating," Kara said, clearly disgusted.

Sheffield laughed. The sound had a particularly nasty ring to it. It was obvious that he hadn't liked the other man. "How about that?"

"Yeah, how about that?" Troy echoed.

"I get my transfer?" Sheffield asked.

Troy's eyes scanned the inmate's less-than-buff physique. If Sheffield worked out, then he was the middleweight champion of the world.

"I'll put the paperwork through myself," Troy promised. He looked at Kara. "Time to hit the road again."

Rather than answer, Kara sneezed as she crossed to the door.

He held it open for her. "Looks like that cold you've been nursing is finally getting the better of you." Outside, the wind was howling. Winter was fighting a knock-down, drag-out fight before giving up its claim on the land. The sky was a gloomy gray. There was going to be more rain on the way. "I'll drop you off at the precinct. Go home, Kara."

She was too tired to argue. Getting into the car, she buckled up. "Where are you going?"

"To pay someone a visit."

Rather than ask who, Kara merely nodded at the information, a sure sign, in his estimation, that she was ill.

An hour later, with Kara on her way home, Troy went to see the late dealer's probation officer. He had questions and maybe she had answers.

She might be a gorgeous woman, he thought as he drove down Aurora's main street to where the county offices were located, but she wasn't exactly at the top of her game when it came to making sure the people assigned to her were clean.

Otherwise, what was Clyde Petrie doing with a gun? A gun that had been turned on him and used to snuff out his life.

He wasn't willing to fully explore the fact that he wanted an excuse, any excuse, to see the probation officer again. She had lingered on his mind like a low, soft melody, the kind whose lyrics insisted on eluding him, but that remained skipping along the perimeter of his thoughts, playing over and over again.

He shook his head. It wasn't as if he was at a loss for female companionship. Since the age of four, he'd enjoyed being around women. They were soft, comforting creatures, each with her own special beauty. He loved them in all shapes and sizes. He loved women and they loved him. And there were no games. Ever. The ground rules were set from the beginning. Enjoyment. Mutual pleasure, nothing less and nothing more. Even though all of his cousins and now even his brothers had decided to pair off, the going-forth-and-being-fruitful route had never been for him. He liked his life, liked his independence. Liked that surge, that excitement of being with someone new.

He saw no reason to give that up. He'd never met a woman who even made him momentarily consider giving it up. But he had to admit that this one was piquing his curiosity.

"Look what the wind just blew in." Jorge uttered the words to Delene as he passed her desk.

She didn't comment. She was too involved with the young woman sitting at her desk, the one whose case had been assigned to her this morning. Rosa Alvarez was hardly more than a girl, really. A girl convicted of prostitution.

Due to some fancy pleading on the part of her court-appointed lawyer, Rosa been placed on probation instead of going to the county jail. The way Delene saw it, Rosa was at a crossroads. She could turn her life around. Or go under. The choice was Rosa's.

Helping the girl was something Delene was bound to do. It was personal. Because there but for the grace of God, Delene thought the moment she looked at the case, went she. Her life could have very easily taken the same wrong turns that Rosa's had. It was obvious to her that the still fresh-faced girl needed someone in her corner. She was going to be that someone.

"Call me." Delene took a white card out of her top desk drawer, wrote her cell phone number across the back, then pressed the card into Rosa's small hand. "Night or day," Delene emphasized. "You need a friend to talk to, call me."

Rosa combed her straight, long dark hair away from her face with her fingers and looked at her with huge eyes. She pressed her lips together, as if she didn't trust her voice for a moment. Instead, Rosa nodded. She tucked the card into the small purse she was clutching.

She had the face of an angel, Delene thought. And wearing the clothes that her attorney had gotten from a secondhand shop in order to make her look more respectable to the judge, she looked like a schoolgirl. Anyone looking at her would have never thought that she was guilty of the crime that had brought her to stand before the judge in the first place. It was both Rosa's appeal, as well as her downfall.

Pushing her chair back, Rosa rose to her feet. "Okay."

She ducked out past Troy, her head down as she avoided making eye contact. In reality, it was a moot point. Troy was too busy looking at Delene.

Belatedly, Delene replayed Jorge's words in her head and looked over her shoulder. Troy's eyes seemed to bore right into hers. A warm shiver danced right between her shoulder blades. He was the last person she expected to see here.

"You always give a hundred and fifty percent of yourself to each of your charges?" he asked her as he sat down.

He made himself right at home, didn't he? she thought, trying not to notice that the air around her seemed several degrees warmer than a moment ago. "I do my best."

Was she really as altruistic as that? Or was it just an act, something he wasn't seeing? "Then what's left over for you?"

She raised her chin defensively. What was he doing here, watching her?

"A feeling of satisfaction." She went on the offensive. "What are you doing here, Detective Cavanaugh? I'm sure you didn't come by to check the status of my emotional reserve."

He would have been by eventually, he admitted to himself now that he was face-to-face with her. Even if work had not sent him here, his curiosity would have. Because although his investigation was finally making some headway, albeit in baby steps, his investigation of one Delene D'Angelo had not progressed at all.

Wanting to find out about her, he'd discovered that there was nothing on her beyond her work record for the past five years and her college transcript. He couldn't even find any record of where she'd lived while she was going to college. The less he found, the more curious he became.

Troy sat back in the chair, allowing himself a moment to appraise her. She had a heart-shaped face and long, dark lashes that were in contrast to her almost platinum hair. He wondered if she was one of those rare creatures, a natural blonde. If her shade came from a bottle, it had been skillfully applied. He caught himself wondering what she would have looked like with longer hair. Her features seemed too fine for the blunt haircut she sported.

"Seems the bullet that came from the gun that killed Clyde was owned by Clyde." He moved forward on the chair until his face was only a matter of inches away from hers. "Since when does the probation department look the other way when it comes to their charges owning guns?"

Tiny flares went up, fueling the uneasiness that was slipping over her. He was too close. Much too close. But to pull back would have highlighted her discomfort. So she willed herself to stay where she was and tried not to dwell on his nearness. Or her reaction.

"We don't," she said coolly. "Are you accusing me of something, Detective?"

Looking at her, he could see her being compassionate. He couldn't see her being sloppy. But how else could they explain Clyde's owning a gun? "Just how thorough are these so-called 'raids' you conduct?"

"Very." The assurance came not from Delene but from Jorge. The man was leaning over the top of the cubicle, glaring at Troy. "When we show up at a place, and by *place,* I mean where they live, where they work, anywhere we feel they might be hiding something, we toss it. They don't get to stash so much as a pinch of cocaine." The big man began to step forward around the cubicle.

Delene held up her hand. She appreciated the thought that motivated Jorge, but she wanted it clear that she could take care of herself. "It's okay, Jorge. I can handle this."

Her colleague looked rather unconvinced, but after a moment he grudgingly retreated to his cubicle. He sent one last malevolent glare Troy's way before he sank down in his seat and out of view.

Troy turned back around to face her. "You've got yourself one hell of a guardian angel there."

She studied him a second to see if he was poking fun at the other man, then decided that he wasn't. And, after all, Jorge couldn't exactly be described using the word *small*.

"You throw mud on one of us, some of it splatters on the rest," she replied philosophically. "Jorge doesn't like mud."

Troy's mouth curved. "Or me, from the looks of it."

No, he probably didn't like the detective, Delene silently agreed. It was a guy thing most likely.

"He's just protective. Jorge told me I reminded him of one of his sisters." Why had she just said that? She was getting too personal. Was this Cavanaugh's way of getting her to drop her guard? *Too bad, I'm on to you.* Her voice took on a professional tone. "We went over every inch of Clyde's place when we raided it the last time. You saw it. He didn't exactly live in the Hearst Castle," she said, referring to San Simeon, a favorite stopping-off place for tourists with a yen to see how the other side once lived. "If Clyde had a gun, he didn't keep it on the premises."

"If not there, then where?" Troy asked. "He didn't exactly strike me as someone who'd own a safety deposit box at your local bank."

"Did it ever occur to you that your source might be lying?"

He shook his head. "No reason for him to do that in this case. It didn't gain him anything to say he sold the weapon to Clyde."

"That you can see," she pressed.

"That I can see," he agreed. This wasn't anything he wanted to lock horns over. He liked to pick his battles and this wasn't one of them. "So, how's your hunt for his daughter going?"

She bit the inside of her lower lip. "Not exactly flying along," she admitted ruefully. "I was going to go back and ask some of the neighbors if any of them saw a woman coming or going from Clyde's motel room since he's been there. If someone has and I can get a sketch artist together with them, then maybe someone will recognize her and come forward—if I can get the drawing circulated."

"Awful lot of 'ifs' there," he pointed out. "Your department's going to fund this?"

What business was that of his? She could feel her back going up again. Why was this detective delving so much into the way she operated? Didn't he have enough work to keep him busy?

"No, I know a sketch artist who owes me a favor. This is on my own time." She couldn't keep her questions to herself any longer. Not when he made no effort to contain his. "You moonlighting for Internal Affairs, Cavanaugh? I thought they only spied on their own people."

The only run-in he'd ever had with Internal Affairs was when Patrick's wife, Maggi, had first come into their lives. But Maggi had since switched departments. He tilted his head slightly as he regarded the woman before him. Did she have something to hide? he wondered yet again.

"Does paranoia come to you naturally," he asked, "or do you have to work at it?"

Good-looking or not, she decided that she didn't

much like this man. She, more than anyone, knew how thin a veneer charm had. "It comes with the territory."

He leaned forward, an easy smile on his lips. "In case you haven't noticed, D'Angelo, I'm not one of your case files."

With effort she clamped down on the flutter that went through her. She forced her mind to focus on the case that had brought the detective here. And when she did, something occurred to her. "What if the gun you're looking for is with Clyde's daughter's mother?"

It took him a second to untangle the possessives she'd thrown at him. When he did, he wondered at the direction this was taking her. "What?"

She sighed. This was so obvious, why hadn't he thought of it? Or did he just want to harass her? "It stands to reason. The only one who would have anything to do with Clyde would have been someone from his own world. A junkie, a prostitute, someone on the lower rungs of life, right? Someone like that deals with lowlife. Maybe once there was a child involved, Clyde thought that mother and daughter might need protection, so he bought the gun for them, not for him."

It was a theory, Troy allowed. "It would have been simpler just to sober up, get a job and get them out of this kind of life."

But she knew better. Knew the way an addict's mind worked better than she would have liked. "No," she contradicted, "it's simpler just to pass a hunk of metal along with a box of bullets to her." He was looking at her strangely. "What?"

"You don't look like the type to be so cynical."

"Like I told you before, Cavanaugh, don't try to pi-geonhole me. I'm not a 'type.'"

Before he could say anything in response, the other man who had been at the motel room with her stuck his head into the cubicle.

"Hey, Delene, the natives are getting restless." Adrian nodded at Troy, then looked back at Delene. "They're lining up for you outside. Standing room only."

Delene looked at Troy. "I've got to get back to work."

He took his cue and rose, still mulling over what she'd just said about Petrie's girlfriend. They needed to find out who she was.

"You might have something there."

"I always do," she said, turning away. Her manner was the last word in confidence, even though she wasn't sure what the man was referring to. She figured asking would cut into her mystique.

There was no need to ask who the man calling him was referring to. Only one "her" interested him and everyone around him knew it.

He couldn't relax. "Where?" Russell barked.

"On camera." Jack Santangelo uttered the words quickly, afraid of angering the man he had called. "It was a news clip."

"You're sure?"

The icy tone cut clear down to the bone. Like the

people he represented, Russell Jackson was not a man
to trifle with.

"I'm pretty sure. I mean, it was just a quick shot, but
it looked like Diane. Yes, yes," Jack tripped over his
own tongue, eager to be done with this, wishing he'd
never called. "It was her."

Russell had been through false alerts before, only
to be disappointed. But he couldn't pass up the chance
that, this time, it was her. "Where is she?"

"In Aurora, California. It's not too far from Sacra-
mento," Santangelo tacked on, since that was where
he'd been sent and he didn't want anyone thinking that
he had skipped out on his assignment. "I was killing
time in my hotel room and just turned on the set. I
caught a glimpse of her. She was hiding behind this
big guy."

An edge came into Russell's voice. "She was with
a man?"

Jack knew enough to be afraid. "More like he was
leading her off. Something about a witness being killed
before he could testify against Miguel Mendoza. You
know, that little detail Anthony sent me out here to
look into."

"Yeah." Details were neither needed nor wanted.
The less said the better. It was a fairly safe bet that
most, if not all, of their conversations were monitored.
Tapes were not admissible in court, but the wrong word
could send those bastards in the FBI heading off in the
right direction, and they were a creative lot. They could

find a way to legitimize their findings so that the judge wouldn't throw them out.

But right now, Russell wasn't thinking in his capacity as the well-paid lawyer for the son of one of the oldest crime families in the country, Anthony Palladino. He was being Russell Jackson, the guy whose wife ran out on him. Nobody said a word around him, but he knew what they were thinking. Knew they were laughing at him behind his back because he hadn't been able to keep his woman where she belonged. Not a day went by these past five years when that didn't gall him. When it didn't eat away at his insides, bit by bit.

He'd spent a considerable amount of time and money trying to find Diane, but it was as if all trace of her had disappeared that day she vanished from the hospital. A hospital room she wouldn't have needed if she hadn't tried to defy him. If she had remained that sweet, meek young woman who had looked up at him with those adoring eyes on their wedding day.

He wanted to get out there, to Aurora. Wanted to take the next flight to the Northern California city. But Anthony had made it known he needed him by his side for the next few days. Things could get hot.

Impatience pawed at his belly like a barely reined-in prize stallion.

"You find out anything else?" he demanded of the caller.

"Not yet, but I wanted to call you and—"

"Find out, damn it. Find out where she's staying. What name she's going by. Everything. Do you hear me? I want every stinking detail. Especially who she's been sleeping with."

Jack Santangelo began to sweat. His bags were packed. His plane ticket back was in his pocket. "But I finished my assignment."

"Then take a vacation," Russell snapped.

"But Anthony—"

He cut Jack off as cleanly as if he'd just used a razor. "I'll take care of Anthony. You find out what you can. I'll be out as soon as this business is finished. Don't leave," he ordered again.

Jack could feel his windpipe tightening as he squeezed the single word out. "Okay."

Dropping the receiver back into its cradle, Russell Jackson smiled for the first time in five years. It was the kind of smile that would have frozen the blood of any man who saw it.

Chapter 7

At the last minute, Delene decided to go home and change before she made the rounds at the Traveler's Motel. She knew that some people found uniforms intimidating, especially ones bearing the insignia of any sort of law enforcement. It was an instant way to create a "them vs. us" barrier that she was looking to avoid.

The only problem was that in civilian garb, she came across as far less authoritative. Only a few steps removed from an old-fashioned, fragile china doll and certainly not to be taken seriously. That was one of the main reasons that she'd made it a point, the moment she was healed, to take classes in the martial arts. She'd become proficient in more than one discipline. That way she would be prepared.

For anything.

For Russell, if he ever came back into her life.

Gravel crunched beneath the soles of her high heels as she made her way to the next door.

Damn, why was she wasting brain matter, thinking about him? He was out of her life for good. The document that she kept in a leather binder said as much. It was a Mexican divorce, obtained in one of those small countries south of the border where anything can be arranged and fixed for a price. The bottom line was that her union to Russell was dissolved. She'd had Russell's copy mailed to him from there, to throw him off as to her whereabouts. It was the last contact she'd had with him.

And then she'd gone on with her life, made something of the bits and pieces that she'd managed to salvage, starting with her self-respect. And now she had a respectable career in a good city. More importantly, she thought as she approached another door, she was making a difference in people's lives.

Except not so much in Clyde's life.

The thought silently mocked her as she knocked. Maybe she hadn't succeeded with Clyde, but that was just going to make her try that much harder with the others. It was a promise she made to herself.

You moved forward or you died. That was something her father had said to her. Just before he left.

The door she'd knocked on opened a crack. The street lamp behind her shone on the chain that was firmly in place. A woman with mousy-brown hair falling into her face looked at her nervously, small brown eyes darting back and forth to see if there was someone else standing behind her. Someone to break down the door.

Sensing her discomfort, Delene immediately offered the woman a reassuring smile.

"Hi, I'm Delene D'Angelo. I'm with the County Probation Department." She held up her identification. The woman squinted at it, as if she needed glasses to make out all the words. "I was wondering if you happened to see a woman entering or leaving Unit 15?" She pointed across the way, where Clyde's room was located.

The brown eyes stared at her, never looking toward where she pointed. "No."

The answer was too automatic. She'd already canvassed the other units and either gotten a negative response, or no one was home. This was her last hope.

"Are you sure?" Delene pressed, trying her best not to come across as desperate as she felt. "It's really important."

The woman's thin face never changed expression. She might have been forty, maybe younger, but life had long been siphoned from her. Delene remembered what that had felt like.

"I mind my own business."

"I'm sure you do," Delene quickly reassured her, "but sometimes you can't help but see things, and if you did see a woman coming out of there, or going in, it could be really helpful."

Evidently the woman on the other side of the door

had long since given up the notion of caring about her neighbor.

"Helpful to who?" There was a touch of defiance in the question, even as she began to close the door.

Delene talked fast. "To a little girl. The dead man had a daughter. I'm trying to locate her. You might have seen her mother."

The woman stopped closing the door and pushed it back to its limit. The chain became taut. "For real?"

"For real," Delene echoed.

The woman pushed her hair from her face as she paused to think. "Saw someone come by with a kid about a month ago. She was a knockout." As she spoke, she became slightly more animated. "The mother, not the kid. Real short skirt, high boots. Cheap but pretty." Something almost begrudging came into her voice as she added, "You know the type."

This had to be the woman she was trying to locate, Delene thought. His girlfriend. Clyde wouldn't have risked trafficking from his room. He knew about the raids, had gone through a couple. He wasn't stupid enough to be found with any kind of drugs in his possession.

"Yes, I do." Delene tried to keep the excitement out of her voice. She didn't want to scare the woman off. "If I brought someone by to sketch her, could you describe the woman you saw?"

The other woman began to retreat again. She didn't want to attract any attention. "Didn't get that good a look."

"Too bad. I'd be willing to pay if you could."

The mention of money brought a dot of color to the pasty complexion. "Well, maybe…" The woman looked at her sharply. "How much?"

Money had always been in short supply except for the years she'd spent with Russell. Then there'd been an unlimited source. She could have bought anything she wanted with it, except for the one thing she desired. Her freedom. Delene thought of what she had in her wallet. It was supposed to last the rest of the week. But this was more important.

"Fifty dollars."

"Make that a hundred." The deep male voice came from behind her.

Startled, Delene swung around. She'd been so intent on getting the woman to trust her, she hadn't heard Troy coming until he was less than two steps behind her.

You're slipping, Dee. You've got to watch yourself.

It took her a second to get her heart rate to slow down to an acceptable beat, but she managed to cover it well. She inclined her head toward Troy. "Detective Cavanaugh."

He smiled broadly at her as he returned the greeting, the tone and the nod. "Agent D'Angelo."

She looked different, he thought. Had it not been for her hair and height, and the fact that he knew she intended to return here to question the residents, he might not have recognized her. There seemed to be an ethereal quality about the woman that she managed to hold somewhat in abeyance when she was in uniform. More than ever, she didn't look like a law-enforcement agent. It was difficult not to stare at her, especially since the light blue turtleneck sweater she wore accentuated the swell of very firm breasts.

He forced himself to focus instead on the woman inside the room. It helped. Some.

"You the police?" the woman behind the door asked. She stared at him with something akin to growing interest.

"One of Aurora's finest."

He slanted a glance toward Delene to see her reaction as he took out his gold shield for the other woman's benefit. From where he stood, Delene seemed annoyed. Probably thought he was cutting in on her territory. He allowed an easy smile to curve his lips. This was one of the neighbors who had been absent when he and Kara had done their initial canvas of the area.

"And we'd be very interested in anything you might have observed about anyone coming or going from that unit over there, ma'am. Unit 15."

Though he'd phrased it innocently enough, even addressing her with respect, the woman obviously took it to mean that he thought she was spying. Thin fingers nervously fluttered around her unwashed hair. She began twisting an end.

"I didn't *observe* nothin'," she insisted. "I was just coming in with my groceries one day and happened to see those two walking in." She looked back at Delene. "The mother and the kid."

"That's exactly what we're after," Troy assured her

smoothly. "If you come down to the station, I can have a sketch artist work with you."

The woman eyed Delene uncertainly. "He with you?"

"We're together," Troy assured the woman quickly.

Too quickly for Delene's satisfaction. She turned her face away from the door so that only Troy could hear her. "In your dreams." She wasn't prepared for his lightning grin to go straight to her gut, but it did.

"You know what they say about dreams, Agent D'Angelo." He winked at her, compounding the felony committed by his grin. "They're only dreams if you can't make them come true."

Her stomach tightened.

This worried her. She couldn't remember the last time she had reacted to a man. That part of her was dead. Or so she'd surmised. Maybe it was just some kind of unavoidable response, like when the doctor taps a certain spot on your knee with a tiny rubber hammer.

She tried to remember that the man annoyed her. Delene blew out a breath. "I don't like you invading my territory."

The twinkle in his eye went to the same spot his wink had. It took all she had not to press her hand to her stomach. God, she hoped she was coming down with the flu.

His voice was low, sultry, as it wrapped itself around her in a whisper meant only for her ears.

"You'll know when I invade, Agent D'Angelo, I promise you that." And then he smiled again, his voice growing louder as he nodded in the potential witness's direction. "Think of this as a hands-across-the-sea joint effort."

Delene had no choice but to go along. The police had every right to be here, while she did not. At least not anymore.

"Right." Delene all but chewed the word up as she spat it out.

The door suddenly closed and she thought they'd lost the woman during their personal locking of horns. But then the door opened again, this time without a chain to tether it in place.

"Okay," the woman announced, throwing a jacket around her painfully thin shoulders. Her hands trembled as she did so. Maybe Clyde had dealt where he lived and this was one of his customers, Delene thought. "I'll come." Standing on the threshold, she moved no farther, eyeing them both. "Where's my hundred?"

Troy placed the full sum into her hand before Delene had a chance to take out her wallet and get her share. Pushing the wallet back into her pocket, she raised a quizzical brow in his direction. He merely smiled in response.

Turning toward the woman, he asked, "Ready?"

For the first time, the thin lips moved back in something that was a close approximation to a smile. "Ready."

"Just exactly what were you doing at the motel?" Delene asked once they had placed the woman, whose name they discovered after some coaxing was Shirley West, together with the department's sketch artist.

Troy watched as Shirley shook her head. The so-called sketch artist, Ron, sat at a computer. He was patiently undoing what he'd just done on the screen and trying again.

"I told you I thought it was a good idea when you mentioned it back at your office. I would have been there sooner, but I had a couple of things to take care of." Troy's eyes shifted to her. "Questioning the residents about Clyde's girlfriend was a lead worth pursuing." He studied Delene for a moment. She looked as if she was about to fidget, but that could have just been his imagination. "You ever think about joining the police department?"

She could keep a relatively low profile where she was. Police work was something else. "I've already got a job."

She was being defensive again, he thought. The lady apparently had a lot of buttons and he seemed to be pressing all of them. "You should never close the door to possibilities."

He was standing much too close again, but that was the fault of the room's layout. Moving away would give away that he made her nervous. She didn't want him thinking that, even if it was true. So she went on the offensive again.

"You're just full of fortune cookie sayings, aren't you?"

Troy crossed his arms before him. "You're trying too hard."

"Too hard?"

"To get me to back off," he elaborated. His eyes met hers. They were more compelling each time he looked at them, he thought. As was she. "Which only makes me wonder why."

She wasn't going to get sucked into any kind of word exchange with this man. She had a feeling he had a great deal of practice. "Maybe I don't like you," she said flatly.

His eyes fairly shone with humor. "Not possible. Everyone tells me I'm very likable."

Anyone else saying that would have come off like a conceited oaf. So why didn't he? Why did she feel an urge to smile? "Maybe they're just lying to you so they don't hurt your feelings."

He leaned over so that his words were only for her. "If they didn't like me, they wouldn't care about my feelings."

This time she did take a step back. His breath along her neck was just too unnerving and distracting. "You do like to argue, don't you?"

His grin broadened, drawing her in. "I like doing other things better."

And it didn't take a brain surgeon to figure out what, she thought.

Something warm and seductive undulated through her, short-circuiting her ability to think clearly. Taking every single inch prisoner. It took more than a little effort for her to break free, even more for her to get her footing back.

She did her best to look at him coldly. "I'm sure you do, but I'm not interested, Cavanaugh."

He inclined his head again, his breath undoing her before the words had a chance. "How do you know unless you try?"

Delene curled her fingers into her hands. This was just a game for him. The kind of game Russell had once played, she reminded herself. It was called conquest. She had to remember that, even if the stakes this time would probably only involve a tumble in the hay.

"Some things you just know," she assured him. "I don't have to jump off a building to know that I wouldn't like what happened once I reached ground level."

"But with a parachute, it might be fun," he pointed out smoothly. She gave him what amounted to a withering look. He didn't retreat. It wasn't in his nature. "All I'm saying Agent D'Angelo is that experiencing the same thing with different people can be—" he winked "—different."

Her stomach did a half gainer. She pressed her lips together, doing her best to show disinterest. "I'll take your word for it," she murmured. Her attention turned to the sketch artist who leaned back at the desk. She read his body language. "I think he might be finished."

"He might be, but I'm not."

He'd said it under his breath as she began to walk away. She'd heard him. And for reasons that Delene couldn't begin to explain or fathom, a small thrill shot through her.

Dammit, she was standing at the edge of a slippery slope. And slippery slopes made you plummet to the bottom. Usually with injuries. And even if there weren't any, she definitely didn't want to start anything with anyone because she didn't want complications in her life. Just maintaining an even keel day to day was difficult enough. She had to focus on surviving. And on being alert. That more than took up her time.

So she turned on her heel to eye him. "Are you threatening me, Detective Cavanaugh?"

He laughed, joining her. The sound made a beeline straight to her gut. Again. She could feel its integrity weakening with each blow.

"I'm probably the most nonthreatening person you'll ever encounter, Agent D'Angelo." Troy made the assurance just before they reached the desk where the sketch artist sat. Shirley was standing over him, looking at the computer monitor. The woman was frowning, twirling the ends of her hair as she cocked her head and stared at the digital rendition.

For a moment, Delene's attention was still on what Troy had just said. "I sincerely doubt that," she muttered under her breath.

He heard her. And grinned. It was yet another assault.

Lights from passing cars played along the interior of his car before they faded out again. He slowed down as he came to a light. After they had dropped off Shirley back at her motel room, he'd once more tried his hand at coaxing Delene out for a drink. Or just a little unstructured conversation at a nearby coffee shop.

She'd said yes to neither. He didn't press any further, but walked her to where she'd parked her car. As he was about to hold her door open for her, a sudden sound from the street had made her cry out and jump. It turned out to be just a car backfiring and she'd regained her composure quickly enough. But just for a split second, he could have sworn he'd detected more than a small trace of fear in her eyes.

What was she afraid of?

Had one of Mendoza's men threatened her? Or did the threat come from one of the myriad hard cases she handled? Someone unhappy with the way she'd interfered with his or her life?

He'd started to ask, but Delene's expression had cut him dead. She was in her car, pulling away before he could get another word out. Almost ran over his feet, he mused with a shake of his head.

His questions were growing more demanding. But the answers still eluded him as much as they had to begin with.

But not for long, he promised himself.

There wasn't a riddle he couldn't solve or a woman whose defenses he couldn't eventually break down, using patience and charm. A little like how he imagined gentling a mustang. It took time, but it was an endeavor that was well worth the effort in the end.

He glanced up at the next sign and realized that he wasn't driving home. He'd driven toward Federal Plaza. The tall buildings that clustered there were sporadically lit. Whole floors were dark, highlighting the scattered lit offices.

One of those offices was near where his sister worked, he thought. Without hesitation, he turned his car toward the central parking lot.

Anytime there was midnight oil burning, his sister would be sitting by it. He showed his identification to the security guard at the ground-floor desk.

Troy then pressed for an elevator. A car arrived almost immediately.

Once in, he pressed for the twenty-first floor, where the D.A.'s offices were located. Janelle needed a life, he thought. Right now, his sister was young, vital and in his opinion the prettiest of all the Cavanaugh women. But she needed to make the most of it. Time had a way of disappearing on you.

His father had said that more than once and they all knew he was thinking about the wife that fate and cancer had taken from him.

"Enjoy every minute," he'd counseled his four children. "You'll never have it again."

Troy smiled to himself as the doors yawned open and he got off. He knew his father was talking about not just enjoying the day, but finding a special someone to enjoy it with. In his case, more than a few women had made his life pleasurable, although just recently work had absorbed most of his time. But he had the capture of a serial killer to show for it.

Janelle, on the other hand, seemed to have lost the knack for fun, he thought as he quietly made his way down the hall until he came to the broom closet she called an office. Because air was scarce, she had the door open.

Several heavy tomes were scattered on her desk, one cover layered over another. Janelle sat, one leg tucked beneath another, her head propped up as she glanced from one page to another. She was frowning.

Definitely lost the knack for fun, Troy thought.

"Can't they chain someone else to the desk and have them do that?"

She looked up as if she'd expected him to come by all along. Very few things startled Janelle. She'd always been the cool one in the family. The one he hated to play against when they played poker.

"They stopped looking once they got to me." Putting down the pen, Janelle rubbed her brow directly above her eyes. There was a knot forming. One that had "headache" written all over it. "Now that we lost that witness we were counting on, we're back to square one with Mendoza." She sighed, turning her chair around to face him. She'd come in early, just before seven. It had been a very long day. "Everyone's too scared to talk. Afraid of being 'taken out,' too."

Troy crossed to her desk and leaned a hip against the side. Janelle scooted some of the books over, away from him. "Mendoza claims he had nothing to do with the murder."

She didn't look as if she quite believed that. Neither did he. "Doesn't really matter who pulled the trigger, Troy. Petrie's just as dead."

"Matters to me."

He was right. Was she really getting to be this jaded? she wondered. Or was she just tired? "Yes, well, it's supposed to matter to you. You're the bright, shining young police detective. You can't have them putting one over on you."

He grinned at her description. "And the bright, shining young assistant district attorney can?"

"Hell no." She nodded at the textbooks on her desk. "The bright, shining young assistant district attorney is desperately searching for a way to stitch this case together even without the testimony of the late, less-than-great Clyde Petrie."

He studied her for a moment, then glanced down at the opened textbooks. "You gonna find it tonight?"

She sighed. "I wish. No," she finally said when she realized that her brother was still waiting for more of an answer.

"Then go home." He straightened, then crossed to the coat rack and got her coat for her. "Better yet, let me take you out to dinner."

She turned around, letting him help her on with her coat. They'd come a long way as brother and sister, she thought, remembering back to when they lived to get one up on each other. "What happened? Someone cancel on you?"

He thought of Delene, then decided not to go there with Janelle. She'd only ask a thousand questions. It was in her nature. "Didn't ask anyone to have them cancel."

Turning, Janelle touched her fingertips to his forehead. "Nope, not burning up. You sure you're my brother? Now that I look—" she pretended to glance behind him "—I don't see that endless line of girls following you."

"There was never an endless line of girls following me. The line was finite," he said, fighting to keep a straight face.

"Even if your ego wasn't." She laughed. She looked one last time at the notes she'd been making. Troy was right. There was nothing there that wouldn't keep until morning. Maybe morning might make them look better. "Okay, you're on, Troy. But you're paying."

"Wouldn't have asked if I wasn't going to."

She hooked her arm through his, then paused to turn off the lights. "Just making sure."

Chapter 8

There were times when Delene felt as if she were running inside a hamster wheel with her foot caught in a spoke, madly trying to just keep up.

No sooner had she banished the demons from her head and closed her eyes than she had to get up again. There was another raid to conduct.

Happily for her, this one did not end in a call to Homicide. Not so happily for the subject of the raid. He was caught in violation of the terms of his probation. Jail time loomed in his future.

Jorge was quick to get out the cuffs. The man whose home they raided, once an up-and-coming CEO of a major company, now reduced to far lesser circumstances, looked at the uniformed trio who had descended upon him. Panic quickly banished disbelief.

"It's just a little weed, man," Ted Addison cried, gesturing at the offending item, which Delene had carefully bagged and tagged. He was standing in his boxer shorts, his knees all but knocking together. Addison glanced from Adrian to Jorge before settling his pleading gaze on Delene. "I just needed it to calm my nerves."

She raised an eyebrow. "What do you have to be nervous about?"

"Raids like this." It looked to Delene as if panic had tightened his throat so that he'd had to squeeze the words out.

He was a man trapped by his own excesses. He had no one to blame but himself for being here, she thought. That still didn't keep her from feeling sorry for him. "Kind of a catch-22, isn't it?" She did her best to sound distant. "You know the rules. No consorting with known felons—"

Still not cuffed, he waved a hand at the bag she was holding. "I got that from a kid in high school. A friend of my son's."

She continued reciting the terms of his particular probation. "No drugs. And weekly meetings of Gamblers Anonymous."

"I've been going to the meetings," the man said, his tone desperate. "Twice a week. Sometimes even three when I'm feeling weak."

Delene tried again. She knew the others were right behind her. Trouble was, she didn't like the position she had to take. "The law says we have to bring you in, Mr. Addison."

"Please?" Addison pleaded with her, as if sensing she was the heart of the group. "Please," he repeated. "I won't do it again."

Delene wavered. Ninety-nine percent of the time she operated by the book. But no one would dispute that Ted Addison definitely had enough on his plate. His wife had left him because of his gambling obsession, taking his sons with her. He was addicted to betting on the horses, had been for a number of years. He'd lost his house and was living in a part of town he would have never even dreamed of visiting before he was laid low by his addiction.

But he still had his job and was honestly trying to turn his life around. He'd been placed on probation when he'd been brought up on charges of check fraud, which in his case translated to bouncing checks. Many of them. To his credit, Addison hadn't attempted to embezzle the money he needed to pay off his debts from his employer. She'd made it a point to check that angle out carefully on her own time.

Sometimes she cared about the people in the files that came across her desk more than they cared about themselves.

Feeling more than a little weary, she blew out a long breath. She made up her mind to take a chance on Addison. Just this one time. "Put the cuffs away, Jorge."

The big man eyed her grudgingly as he tucked the steel bracelets into his back pocket.

"Oh, thank God," Addison cried, his voice hitching in a suppressed sob.

She regarded him coldly. "The next time we come—and there will be a next time, Mr. Addison—you'd better be so clean, you squeak."

He held up his hand. It was trembling, as was he. "I promise."

Delene handed the small bag of evidence over to Jorge while Adrian looked on. "Flush that down the toilet, Jorge."

He took the baggy from her, looking at first it, then her dubiously. "You sure about this?"

"Yeah, I'm sure." She knew that Jorge would go along with her. So would Adrian. She wanted both men to understand her reasoning. "He only had the one joint." They had tossed the premises pretty thoroughly. "Can't see ruining a man's life and sending him to jail over something so minor." In some states in the country, with the right condition, Addison would have been written a prescription for the substance. And after all, it wasn't as if the man was dealing, she thought.

Addison grasped her hands between his. If she'd allowed him, he would have kissed them. "Thank you. Thank you."

She drew her hands away. "You have one chance, Mr. Addison. Don't blow it," she warned.

Once they left the premises and were back on the street, Adrian broke rank. He was the first to the car parked by the curb.

"I could have stayed in bed," he complained. He yanked open the passenger door behind the driver's seat.

Delene watched Jorge open his side before she got in. She was riding shotgun today. Jorge had the driver's side. They made it a point to rotate for each raid.

"Then we wouldn't have put the fear of God into Addison and who knows, in a couple of weeks or more, he might have gone on to something bigger, something worse," Delene pointed out.

Jorge stuck his key into the ignition as Adrian leaned forward, his hands on the back of Jorge's seat. "Got an answer for everything, don't you?"

She only wished, Delene thought. "Yeah," she answered cheerfully, "I do."

The phone rang five times before she had a chance to reach for the receiver and pick it up. Hip-deep in paperwork she'd neglected, she mumbled an almost belligerent "D'Angelo."

"Thought you might want to know that we might have a name for Petrie's girlfriend."

Instantly alert, her back went ramrod straight. She recognized his voice instantly. It went through her like a stream of hot water, warming everything in its path. "Someone recognize the sketch?" she heard herself asking. Not bad for a woman who felt as if she'd been struck dumb.

"Actually, I did." Troy thought of toying with her a

little, drawing out the moment, but he knew that she wouldn't appreciate it. He backtracked a little before explaining his answer. "Petrie's room was dusted for prints. Latent almost went crazy because there were so many given the type of room it was, but one of the partials they came up with belonged to a Kathy Springer. Seems she's in the system. Convicted of prostitution when she was eighteen, then again when she was twenty." It was a sad history, but not an unusual one given the area they were dealing with. "She's pretty much fallen off the radar after that. When I pulled up her picture, she was a dead ringer for the drawing that neighbor had our man compile."

Something inside Delene cheered. "No known address?" She knew it was almost too much to hope for.

"Nothing current," he confessed. "We're still working on it." Silence met his answer. "You still there, Agent D'Angelo?"

She was trying to piece things together. "This Kathy has a daughter. Kids need to see doctors. Which means that Kathy and the girl might be on Medicaid."

Troy laughed dryly. "Last I checked, they weren't issuing health care cards to street prostitutes."

A child made a difference in a person's life. At least some of the time. "Maybe she cleaned up her act long enough to apply for public assistance."

"Worth a look," Troy agreed. There was a short pause on the other end of her line, as if he was waiting for something. And then she heard him say, "This is where you're supposed to say 'You done good, Detective Cavanaugh.'"

"'You done good, Detective Cavanaugh,'" she parroted, but he was almost positive he heard a smile in her voice. It was enough to have him press his next move.

"So, does this earn me a cup of coffee?"

She pressed her lips together, holding back an unexpected laugh. She couldn't say why his relentlessness tickled her. At least part of the time. "You can have coffee anytime you like."

She knew what he meant, Troy thought. But since she gave no indication that she was about to make the offer, he said, "With you."

He made it sound as if he'd done this strictly for her. She knew better. "Aren't you just working on your own case, Detective?"

"Yes," he allowed, "but nowhere does it say that I have to share my findings with an agent from the County Probation Department."

"No," she agreed slowly, "it doesn't." She paused, debating. In a way, she did owe him for this, even though it had been her idea to look for the girlfriend to begin with and she'd had a different reason to go searching for the woman. But she didn't like owing anyone. "Okay, I suppose it can't hurt."

She heard him laugh. "I promise it'll be utterly painless."

Delene sincerely had her doubts about that. But she gave him instructions as to where to meet her anyway.

* * *

"Am I boring you?" Troy finally asked when she yawned again.

They had met in a coffee shop a block away from the building where the County Probation Department was housed. So far, by his count, she'd yawned three times and he hadn't even finished his cup of coffee.

A soft shade of pink he found endearing entered her cheeks as Delene waved away his question with her hand. "Sorry, I didn't get much sleep last night and I had a raid this morning."

A lot of people were inside the coffee shop, and it felt as if the air supply had been depleted. That and the press of warm bodies made her struggle to keep her eyes open.

She'd just trampled on his ego, she thought as she set her cup down on the saucer.

Troy studied her for a moment, leaning in to be heard above the din of voices and the shuffle of feet and chairs. "That a pretty regular thing?"

She shrugged. "To a fair extent."

"You should get hazard pay." His smile faded a little to be replaced by a look that resembled concern. "Why are you having trouble sleeping?"

"I didn't say I had trouble sleeping," she pointed out tersely. "I just said I didn't get much sleep last night."

He had a feeling that he'd phrased his question correctly despite her protest, but he wasn't about to push it. He played along. "Okay, what was different about last night?"

Nothing, she thought. It was like every other night she'd spent these past five years. She would come home after a long day, make sure all her windows were locked, then would look into her closet and under her bed like a paranoid ninety-year-old woman. After which she'd have a meager, lackluster meal and flop into bed. Where she would lie awake, magnifying every single noise she heard until sometime during the night she'd fall into a fitful sleep. Last night the nightmare had come again, in a slightly different form, but all the basic elements had been the same. Enough to make her afraid long before she opened her eyes.

But Cavanaugh was waiting for an answer and she sure as hell wasn't going to give him the truth. "I was just preoccupied with finding Clyde's daughter while juggling the rest of my case files. That takes a lot out of you."

He had a feeling she had more than enough to give. After finishing his coffee, he set the cup down, not willing to leave just yet. He wanted to know more, anything she was willing to share.

"So how did this morning's raid go? Since we didn't get in a call, I take it the subject of this raid turned out to be breathing."

She grinned without realizing it. "Inhaling actually."

It took him a second to draw his eyes away from her expression. He felt like a man in a trance. Or a man who'd just been kicked where he lived. By a mule with heavy iron horseshoes.

"Come again?"

"The guy we were raiding was smoking marijuana."

Nodding as he took in the information, Troy drew the logical conclusion. "So he was busted."

When he saw Delene bite her lower lip, something stirred in his belly. He had a sudden urge to do the same, to gently chew on her lower lip and sample the taste of her mouth. No doubt about it. The more he saw the lady, the more he wanted to see her. And to win her over.

He'd never felt quite this determined before.

Because she wasn't answering, he revised his guess 180 degrees. "He wasn't busted?"

Delene shrugged, looking away. Troy reached across the small table, putting his hand over hers to get her attention. She jumped, pulling back as if he'd just burned her.

"I'm not wearing a wire, Delene. I'm not here to trap you," he assured her. "You can trust me."

It was the first time he'd used her first name. He was getting much too personal. She needed to resurrect the space between them. "I don't make it a habit to trust anyone, Detective Cavanaugh."

But he saw something in her eyes. Something that spoke to the very core of him. Something vulnerable. And he wanted to protect her. To make her feel safe even if she wouldn't admit that she felt exposed.

"Don't you think it's about time you called me something a little less formal than Detective Cavanaugh?"

Her eyes met his. She refused to give an inch, knowing if she did, she'd be losing a mile. "No."

"Okay." He inclined his head indulgently. "I can wait."

Her eyes narrowed. Most other men would have walked out by now. Or at the very least, uttered a curse and written her off. "Why?"

"Why what?"

He was smiling at her. Damn him, why did he have to have such a sexy smile? She could feel its effects right down to the pit of her stomach, to the ends of her toes. She blamed it on not having made love in five years. More. It had been so long, she wasn't even sure if any of the equipment involved still worked.

"Why would you wait? Why are you bothering?" she demanded, her tone rising along with her ire. "Is this some kind of a conquest thing with you, Cavanaugh?" She deliberately used his last name to let him see that no headway was made. "Do you have to break down the resistance of every woman in the world?"

"That's not fair," he protested and then flashed a wide grin she knew any woman with a pulse would have found irresistible. "I haven't met every woman in the world."

Delene pushed her chair back, narrowly avoiding bumping it against the back of another. "I have to get back."

He caught her by the wrist before she could turn from the table. His grip was easy, but firm. "What the hell are you running from, Delene?"

Her chin shot up. She felt herself spoiling for a fight. It made things easier. "Who says I'm running?"

His grip remained fast. "For one, the track marks across my body every time I try to get to know you a little better."

"Don't try," she told him firmly. "Get it through your head, Detective Cavanaugh, I'm not interested. I know that must seem hard for you to accept, given your looks and your track record with women, but I am not interested," she repeated.

"Number one, I'm not proposing marriage here—"

Her eyes clouded over until they looked like the sky just before a thunderstorm. "I'm not interested in a roll in the hay, either."

He glossed over her words as if she hadn't even said them. "Number two, how would you know anything about my so-called 'track record' unless you've been asking questions about me, which would indicate at least a mild interest on your part?"

"*Interest* is the wrong word, Cavanaugh." Then, before he could say anything to contradict her, she continued. "If I had a snake in my backyard, I'd sure as hell be asking people questions about how to get rid of it." Delene silently dared him to put a positive spin on what she'd just said.

Instead of commenting on her less-than-flattering analogy, he shrugged, deliberately taking no offense. "Again, what are you afraid of?"

"Detectives who won't take no for an answer."

He looked at her for a long moment, still holding on to her wrist. Then slowly Troy opened his fingers, releasing her. Surprised, Delene grabbed up her purse again, ready to make a quick retreat. She had just cleared the table when he said something to stop her in her tracks.

"Who are you, Agent D'Angelo?"

Because a couple of people around the table were staring at them, she sank back down in the seat she'd vacated, her tone dropping as her knees did. "Is this some kind of philosophical question?"

"No, it's a very basic question, really." He watched her expression, her eyes, confident that he could pick up any telltale sign of lies. "There's no record of you that goes back beyond five years."

She knew better than that. She'd overseen its addition herself. "There's my college transcript."

"And only that." Brenda, Dax's wife, had told him it was no great obstacle to change the name on the transcript.

When Delene looked at him quizzically, he elaborated. "No clubs you might have joined, no canceled checks paying for your rent or schoolbooks. No charge card receipts." It was as if she hadn't existed outside of the university halls—*if* she'd actually attended there in the first place.

Delene met his gaze head-on. She'd prepared this answer long before he had ever come on the scene. "I didn't have time for clubs, I was too busy with school and work. And I always paid in cash."

"How?" he wanted to know. "There's no employment record dating back across that time to coincide with your social security number."

She was ready for this, too, like lobbing tennis balls back over the net. "I was paid under the table. It was a research project," she added before he could ask.

He still had a question. "What project?"

The man made her think of a relentless machine, unable to stop coming no matter what. "It folded."

The hell it did, he thought. She'd made it up. The whole thing. "There's no driver's license dating back beyond five years," he pointed out.

She spread her hands wide, her face the picture of innocence. "Didn't drive."

Troy looked at her. Her expression was immovable. What she maintained could be possible. But it was highly improbable.

"At first I thought you might have been in the witness protection program, but that didn't seem right. What would you be doing working for the county in that case? That kind of job would be too high profile for someone who might have given evidence against someone important enough to have landed you in this setup. Then I thought that maybe you were working undercover."

Delene pulled her purse more tightly to her as she laughed shortly. "For five years?"

"Deep cover," he emphasized. He'd explored that avenue, too, thanks to a few informants, and had come up empty. "But there aren't any irregularities within the department big enough for you to explore this intently."

"How would you know?" She leaned forward, a

mocking expression on her lips. "Or are you clairvoyant, too?"

"No," he answered easily, "but I'm a Cavanaugh. That means I've got an unlimited supply of eyes and ears out there, collecting information for me. You may not know this, but there are a lot of avenues to tap into to find out about a public servant. But all the avenues led nowhere. I couldn't find out anything about you, Agent D'Angelo, except that you're one of the most intriguing, most attractive women I'd ever come across."

Flattery, empty flattery. She'd been here before. "And you want to go to bed with me."

A smile slowly curled along his lips. There was no point in denying it. She wouldn't believe him anyway. And there was something to be said for the truth. "The thought has crossed my mind."

"So, it's just sex."

He studied her for a moment. She thought she saw amusement in his eyes and took offense. It was safer than falling into the hole that look created.

"I take it your homework on me wasn't very thorough, either. It's never 'just sex' when I'm with a woman, Agent D'Angelo. There's always a lot more involved."

Suddenly she felt as if she were sitting on a sailboat made of tissues. She took the offensive again. "Do you give references, too?"

He laughed. "That would be telling, and a gentleman never tells."

"I wasn't aware that you knew what the word *gentleman* meant."

He leveled a gaze at her that pinned her in place. "That's not fair."

No, she supposed it wasn't. But she didn't feel very much like being fair. Not when she was under attack. Not when she felt herself in the very real danger of losing the battle. Because somewhere during this little exchange they were having, she'd realized that she wanted to go to bed with Troy Cavanaugh probably just as much as he wanted to go to bed with her.

Maybe more.

Chapter 9

Mayday!

The urgent cry echoed through Delene's brain over and over again. Now that he was no longer holding on to her wrist, she knew it was time to get up from the table. Common sense told her she should be walking away from Cavanaugh and out of the coffee shop as quickly as possible. Before she found herself in danger again.

In danger of what? Of coming under someone's thumb again? That was never going to happen and she knew it. She was too distrustful, too vigilant for that to be a real threat. She wasn't nineteen and impressionable anymore.

In danger of falling in love again? Fat chance, she

sneered silently. To love someone, she had to be able to feel something, and as far as she was concerned, she was pretty much dead inside. Russell had conducted a scorched-earth policy through her soul, making it impossible for her to feel anything for anyone, other than perhaps a little compassion. Love didn't enter into the picture. And trust was a big factor here. To love, she would have had to trust—and she trusted no one.

That left her only with a physical reaction. She supposed she was only human. Humans reacted to stimuli and Detective Troy Cavanaugh was nothing if not stimulating.

She looked at him for a long moment, debating her next move. Retreat? Or charge?

If you entered a dark room and you thought your imagination was going to run away with you, see things that weren't there, you'd turn on a light, right? A light that illuminated all the corners, broke up all the menacing shadows. You'd take action, you wouldn't remain in the dark, huddling in fear.

If she walked away from this now, a part of her was still huddling in fear. She'd come too far for that to be true.

Still looking at Troy, Delene squared her shoulders like a warrior on the battlefield, about to engage in combat. Ready to dispel the shadow of attraction and send it into her past.

"Detective Cavanaugh, would you like to come over tonight?"

Troy stared at the woman across from him. Was he hallucinating?

Had he still been sipping his coffee, he had a feeling the black liquid would have found its way out again in a less-than-fine spray. She was kidding, right? Baiting him.

Each time they ran into each other, Delene D'Angelo had parried and blocked his every attempt to get close to her. There might have been more than the usual amount of attraction humming between them, but there was also a barbed-wire fence separating them, and that put a rather large crimp in his getting to know her.

There had to be something he wasn't getting.

Had he been a resident of the ancient city he'd been named after, a name that had been heaped on his shoulders because his mother had been reading *The Iliad* when he was born, he still would have been one of the people voting against taking the huge wooden horse inside the city walls.

At least not until it had been carefully examined.

On the surface, the invitation sounded simple, very blatant. But the woman extending it wasn't either simple or blatant. Troy was cautious when it came to traps.

So rather than accept, he moved forward on his seat, looked her right in the eyes and asked, "Is this a test, Agent D'Angelo?"

Delene smiled. "No test."

He was far from convinced. "If I said yes," he began, "what would the next words out of your mouth be?"

She gave him a straight answer. "I'd talk about a mutually acceptable time."

His expression didn't change. "Just like that?"

Neither did hers, but inside, she had to admit that she was somewhat amused, not to mention amazed that he didn't jump at the opportunity, seeing as how she was convinced that sleeping with her had been his goal right from the beginning. Men like Cavanaugh were all alike.

And yet he wasn't saying yes. "Just like that," she echoed.

He wasn't buying it. There had to be something behind it. Was she working with Internal Affairs, after all? But he had no reason to suspect that the department would find anything wrong with two consenting adults consenting.

What the hell was going on? "You've stonewalled me at every turn, made me feel as if I was attempting to tread on holy ground in muddy combat boots every time I began to get a little personal and now, all of a sudden, you're inviting me to your apartment."

When she was satisfied that he was finished, she nodded. "Pretty much what you just said, yes."

"Okay, so what's the catch?"

She knew that the more innocent she looked, the more suspicious he would probably be, but she didn't know any other way to state this. "No catch."

He eyed her more closely. Maybe she was just inviting him over, nothing else. No, she wasn't ten. She had to know the implication behind her words. Didn't she? "You are saying what I think you're saying?"

It felt nice to have the clear upper hand with him for a change. Her mouth curved as she played out the moment, trying not to wander off into those two dimples gently indenting his cheeks. Her heart fluttered before she could stop it.

"What do you think I'm saying?"

He took a breath, then drawled, "That somewhere along the line during the evening, clothing will become optional."

She heard herself laugh. The sound took her by surprise. As did he. Troy Cavanaugh wasn't nearly as crass as she'd first thought he was. In addition, he had a way of phrasing things that took the edge off the situation and yet made things tighten in anticipation all through her body.

"Yes," she said softly, so that there would be no doubt. "That's what I'm saying."

Anticipation had the very tips of his fingers tingling. She was a lady he was going to deeply enjoy pleasuring. But there was still something he had to know. "Why the sudden change of heart?"

She shifted, uncomfortable with the term he'd used. "Heart has nothing to do with this, Detective Cavanaugh. This is just about sex."

The hell it was. His eyes held hers. If there was a way of finding out the truth, it would mean looking into her soul. "Not that I have anything against 'just sex,' mind you, but you thought that was all it was before. What changed?"

She was brutally honest in her answer. As it was, she was living enough of a lie. "I decided that it's best to meet things head-on instead of letting them fester."

Fester. Now there was an image to keep in your head when you were making love. He laughed, shaking his head. "You do like to sweet-talk a man, don't you?"

She hadn't thought it was going to take this much convincing. She hadn't thought there would be any convincing at all once she made her proposition. She decided to let him know exactly what she was thinking. "We're attracted to each other."

"Yes," he agreed.

"That attraction keeps coming up, getting in the way of the investigation." She didn't add that it was getting in the way of her thinking process, as well, because she was only just now admitting that to herself.

Troy grinned. The dimples deepened. "I thought it was adding a nice little coda. Not that I'm not intrigued by your offer." He held up his hands to forestall any thought of her rescinding the invitation.

"It's not an offer. It's a suggestion," she corrected. "A way for us to move on and put this thing completely behind us."

She made it sound only slightly more palatable than drinking hemlock. "We *are* talking about making love here, right?" He peered up at her face. "And not a proctology exam."

"We're talking about having sex," she said. "What time's good for you?"

It took effort for him not to laugh. She seemed too dogged about this, almost clinical. "Just about any time you mention," he told her. His eyes swept over Delene's face slowly as he took full measure of what she was saying.

Something quivered inside of her. She ignored it. "Seven o'clock all right with you?"

"Do you mean a.m. or p.m.? Not that it matters," he explained, his voice feathering over her despite the crowded conditions of the coffee shop, "but I don't want to show up at the wrong time."

"I meant p.m." Damn it, why were her insides suddenly decomposing to the consistency of Jell-O? "I said tonight," she reminded him, biting off the words.

"Just getting my facts straight." He stared at her for a long moment. The smile on his face faded a little. "You're serious, aren't you?"

"Aren't you?"

Part of him still thought she was either baiting him, or just bantering. A warmth spilled through his loins now that he gave the matter real thought.

"Not if I can help it," he told her. "My work is serious enough, the rest of my life I try to keep as light as possible."

Troy glanced at his watch. He had to be getting back, even though he would have preferred to remain here, talking to her like this. Part of him believed that he was having a nice dream and that, sadly, it would end the moment he walked out of the coffee shop. But the work wouldn't do itself and if Kara had to handle the workload, he knew he would never hear the end of it.

On the off chance that she actually *was* serious, he said, "So I'll see you tonight at your place at seven."

"Yes."

There wasn't a glimmer of a smile on her face. He had to believe she was serious. And if she was serious, he still didn't understand why. Her excuse didn't really hold water.

Or did it?

He shook his head. "You are an unusual woman, Agent D'Angelo." He paused for a moment, then asked, "Do I get to call you Delene tonight?"

She told herself that if she relinquished the shield provided by her title, that wouldn't make any of this more personal. Delene really wasn't her name anyway, even though it was what she'd answered to these past five years. "If you want to."

Bits and pieces of tonight's scenario began to play through his head. "And you'll call me Troy?"

She felt as if the ground beneath her feet was turning into quicksand. Maybe this wasn't the smartest thing she'd ever done. She did her best to keep a poker face in place.

"If that's what you want."

What he wanted was to bring color back to her face, sparkle into her eyes. What he wanted was to make tonight the most memorable night she had ever experienced.

"That's what I want." Leaving her with a wink, he turned away and started to walk toward the front entrance.

He took exactly three steps before the annoying tones of his cell phone emanated from his pocket. He stopped and took it out, then flipped it open. Because there was a low level of noise around him, he covered his other ear. "Cavanaugh."

"Where are you, pretty boy?" Kara's voice came through the phone loud and clear. She sounded slightly impatient.

They usually took lunch together. Kara didn't like to eat alone. "Having coffee at The Coffee Express. Want anything?"

"Yeah, for you to get your butt down to Central and Grand."

Was she being petulant because he'd ducked out on her? "You want me to stand in the middle of the crosswalk?"

"No, wise guy, I want you to meet me in front of the Grand Hotel." He was familiar with the place. It was anything but what its name indicated. The run-down, seedy establishment was home to a number of people down on their luck, hoping to move up, afraid that they might be moving down. "One of *my* informants came through." Kara took the opportunity to crow because most of the time, despite her time on the force, most sources turned out to be his. "We've got a possible Kathy Springer sighting, thanks to someone I know in the Medicaid department. You interested? Or do you want to have another cup of rip-off designer coffee?"

"I'm on my way."

After snapping the phone shut, he tucked it back into his pocket and started toward the door again. But as he waited for a couple to make their way out ahead of him, he hesitated. He and Kara wouldn't have even been looking for Kathy Springer if it hadn't been for Delene. She was the one looking for the woman to begin with.

He knew that later he could tell Delene where Kathy was, after they'd taken the woman in for questioning. But Delene had made it clear that she wanted to be the one to break the news to the woman and her daughter. This was a homicide case, not a matter up for show-and-tell. Which meant that he should just keep walking. But to be a good cop didn't mean always strictly playing by the rules. Listening to his brothers talk about their cases had taught him that.

Even his father bent a rule or two when the time called for it.

He made his decision.

"Got gum on your shoe?" Just as he was about to turn around and go back, Delene came up to him. "You're stuck in place," she pointed out.

Someone jostled against her, sending her all but into his arms. It took a second before they both backed up again. His racing pulse was a new sensation. He summoned a great deal of restraint not to kiss her. "We found Kathy Springer."

Surprise, then pleasure slipped over her features.

There was a light in her eyes that he found particularly inviting.

"Great," she cried. "Where?" As an afterthought, in case he had any ideas about making a quick retreat, she took his arm.

The contact surprised him. She was physical when she got excited, he thought. Good to know. "The Grand Hotel on Grand and Central. I'm on my way over there now. Want a ride?"

She wanted to be able to stay with Kathy and her daughter if she had to. Besides, she didn't like being dependent on someone else. "I've got my own car. I'll follow you."

It might be better that way, Troy decided as he finally went to the parking lot. He watched and waited while Delene got into her car and then brought it around behind his. As he pulled out of the lot, Delene stayed with him. If they arrived in their own vehicles, it wouldn't look to Kara as if he'd actually brought Delene to the site.

For about a minute and a half, he mocked himself, bracing for the lecture Kara would feel bound to deliver. The one about secrecy and ongoing investigations.

Traffic conspired against their making good time. Ten miles took over thirty minutes. He and Delene pulled into the hotel's limited parking lot almost at the same time. Once they emerged from their respective cars, he could see the frown on Kara's face from where he was. He was going to have to do some placating later on. Maybe offer to do some of her paperwork in order to smooth her ruffled feathers.

"Sorry, traffic was bad," he said to his partner as he approached.

The frown on Kara's face did not recede. She paused only long enough to blow her nose. Her cold had her in a bad mood.

"Bringing along your own cheering section these days?" she asked, giving Delene the once-over.

His tone cut short any sarcasm Kara might have had to offer. "Have you talked to the superintendent yet?" he asked.

Kara shook her head. "No, I wanted to wait for you first."

Troy opened the door to the small, dark foyer. The smell of ammonia permeated the air. A stoop-shouldered man in a green shirt and darker green pants was listlessly pushing a mop around. The water in the pail beside him was murky.

Unable to contain herself any longer, Kara hissed into Troy's ear. "Why is she here?"

Despite his partner's judgmental tone, Troy couldn't help smiling. Kara was the last person on earth to be considered for the post of goodwill ambassador. Her people skills left a great deal to be desired.

"Delene was with me at the coffee shop when I got your call."

The mildest trace of interest flittered across Kara's brow. She looked at Delene again. They were all inside the building now. The man mopping the floor had his back to them, ignoring them as he worked.

"So?" Kara pressed, still not seeing the connection. Or the need for Troy to bring the woman along, even if she might have been his latest source of interest.

Delene had no intentions of standing quietly by as they talked around her. She had just as much right to be here as they did.

She spoke up. "So, if it wasn't for my looking for Clyde's girlfriend in order to find his daughter, you people might not have even thought to look for her."

Troy tried to cut through any further questions from Kara. "Professional courtesy," he explained. "I owe her one."

Kara frowned, clearly not happy, but still not about to make waves for a partner she respected and worked well with. "You could have just sent a thank-you card."

Humor glinted in his dark blue eyes. "Next time."

The words had come from Troy, but they made a cold shiver run down Delene's back. Next time? Was he making plans? She didn't want plans, didn't want anyone thinking they had the right to make plans that involved her or feeling as if they had any say over her life at all.

The only one who had a say in her life was her, and it was going to stay that way.

"There's not going to be a next time, Cavanaugh," she informed him tersely.

Kara's mouth dropped open and then she smiled. Broadly. Amusement and pleasure danced in her eyes as she looked at her partner. "She's not interested in you, pretty boy. I didn't think there was a woman alive who wasn't interested in you."

Delene blew out a breath. She had called in to the office and taken a few hours' personal time. She didn't want to waste it standing here, listening to Cavanaugh's partner cackle.

"Do you think you could see your way clear to not talking about me as if I wasn't here?"

For the first time, Kara grinned at her. "Sorry, my fault. Won't happen again." She hummed to herself as she led the way to the man with the mop. Tapping him on the shoulder, she waited until the slight, dark-haired man looked at them.

Both Kara and Troy showed him their badges. "Detectives Cavanaugh and Ward," Troy said. He shoved his wallet back into his back pocket. "We're looking for someone in connection to a homicide." The moment he said the word, the superintendent's ruddy complexion turned pale.

"I run a clean place," the man declared, clutching his mop with both hands.

"I'm sure you do," Troy said mechanically. "Do you have a Kathy Springer staying here?"

He thought for a moment, then shook his head. "Nope, can't say that I do."

Troy glanced at Kara. The woman moved forward, unwilling to accept the man's answer. "She's blonde, skinny, has a little girl with her. About four or five."

Still the man shrugged and shook his head again.

"They come, they go. As long as they pay their rent on time and don't make noise after eleven, I don't really notice them."

Troy felt his pockets, but the photograph he had of Kathy, reprinted from the mug shot they found, wasn't in any of them. He looked at his partner. "Did you bring a picture of her?"

Kara shook her head, chagrined. "I didn't think to bring it," she confessed. "You?"

He thought back, then remembered where it was. "On my desk at the precinct."

"Damn," Kara muttered. "Look, she's about—"

Before she could continue with the description, Delene elbowed her way in. She held up a photograph, the one she'd copied from Kathy's driver's license.

"How about her?" she asked the superintendent. "Have you seen this woman? Is she staying here?"

Leaning the mop handle against the wall, he wiped his hands against his coveralls and then took the photograph from her. He peered at it closely, squinting in order to focus better.

And then he nodded, his head jerking up and down like one of those ceramic bobble heads.

"Yeah, sure, I know her. That's Serena Sherman. She's in 2B." The superintendent handed the photograph back to Delene. "New here. Keeps to herself. And she's got a kid. Kinda thin, but very pretty." There was a touch of a leer to his lips as he watched Delene put away the photograph again. "Like her mother."

"In 2B," she repeated. "Thanks, that's all we need." Turning to Troy and his partner, she smiled. "Looks like we're all in business again."

Chapter 10

Troy could hear Delene exhale an impatient breath directly behind him as he knocked on the door of 2B for a third time. There was still no answer.

"She's not home," Kara said. "Let's go."

Just then the door opened. The woman who looked at them with accusing eyes was not Kathy Springer. Or Serena Sherman. Not unless the woman in the photograph had suddenly aged about forty years and gained close to a hundred pounds.

Scowling, the woman in the bright, crisp lavender-and-green floral housecoat planted herself in the doorway, her body prohibiting any access into the apartment.

"Quiet," she rasped, annoyance etched into her features as she glanced over her shoulder. A television set was on behind her. The program she'd been watching had gone to a commercial break. Troy had a hunch that was the only reason she'd come to answer the door. "You'll wake up the baby."

"Baby?" Delene echoed. The little girl in the photograph she'd seen in Clyde's motel room had been around four or five. Had the superintendent given then the wrong apartment number?

The woman shrugged, then inserted her hand beneath the housecoat to fix a bra strap that had slipped from her shoulder.

"Well, she's really four, but I call her 'baby' because, hell, at my age, almost anyone under twenty is a baby." Then, as if she suddenly realized she was becoming friendly with strangers, she scowled again, looking at Troy since he towered over all of them. "What do you want?"

Troy took out his badge and showed it to her. "I'm Detective Cavanaugh. This is my partner, Detective Ward." He glanced to see that Kara was holding up her identification.

Leaning forward and squinting, the woman made it a point to look at both badges. Satisfied that they were real, she nodded toward Delene. "Who's that?"

Delene already had her identification out. "I'm Delene D'Angelo. I'm with the County Probation Department."

The woman's brow knitted together, as if she was

digesting the information. "Serena done something wrong?" she asked.

Troy wasn't about to go into any detail. "I'm sorry," he said politely. "I didn't catch your name."

The woman straightened her somewhat bulk-encumbered frame, annoyed that she hadn't gotten an answer. "That's because I didn't throw it. I'm Louise Patton. I babysit for Serena when she's working."

Troy turned toward Delene. "Give me the photograph you showed the super." She did as he asked and he took it from her, showing it to the woman. "Is this Serena?"

"Yeah, that's her." Her head bobbed as she once again glanced over her shoulder. The parade of commercials was still going on. She returned her attention to the people in the hallway. "But she's not home right now."

"Where is she?" Kara asked.

The woman's small, deep-set brown eyes moved from one to another slowly. Missing nothing. "What's this all about?"

Troy paused for a moment, debating how much to share with the woman. "We'd like to speak to Serena in regards to a homicide investigation."

Every bone in Louise's body seemed to snap to attention. Drama had left her television set and the realm of make-believe and had come calling into her life. "Who's dead?"

Troy's smile was easygoing. And immovable. "We'd like to speak to Serena first."

Louise Patton gave an unladylike snort and looked properly annoyed at being kept in the dark. Delene would have been willing to bet one month's pay that the woman was a regular nonstop gossip when it came to her friends and neighbors. Louise struck her as someone who desperately needed to know everything about the people around her.

"Would you know where she is?" Troy pressed gently. More gently than the situation warranted, given his position, Delene thought. She knew a lot of policemen liked to throw their weight around, and he should have been more inclined than most, given his pedigree. That he didn't gave her pause. And made her see him in a more favorable light.

It further undermined the feelings she wanted to have about him.

Louise's wide shoulders rose and fell in lieu of a verbal claim of ignorance. "Said she had some errands to run, and then she's going to go to work. She's usually gone from around seven."

"Do you know where she works?" Delene addressed the question to the back of Louise's head. There were several places where the roots were coming back, with more than a touch of gray.

The woman was checking up on her program. A second battery of commercials had come on, delaying her viewing even longer.

Turning back around, she shook her head in response to the question. "No, she don't tell me." The corners of her mouth rose in a superior fashion. "But I've got my suspicions." And then she jerked her shoulders up and down again. "But she pays me every morning when she comes home, so I can't complain. I've got insomnia," she confided. "Might as well make some money while I look for something decent enough to watch on TV."

Troy had a feeling that given enough time, Louise Patton would tell them everything she'd ever known about anyone or anything. For her talking was as natural as breathing.

"She works until morning?" Kara asked just before she sneezed.

The woman seemed irked that she was expected to repeat herself and disdainful that the detective was sneezing in her presence. "That's what I said."

"What time does she come home?" Delene asked.

The babysitter thought a moment. "Sometimes at two, sometimes at four. It's not like she punches in a clock here." She cackled before adding on smugly, "Easy money for me—her daughter's an angel."

The endless march of commercials was finally over and it was obvious that she wanted to get back to watching her program. One hand on the door, Louise began to shift impatiently, eager to close it.

"You got a card or something I can give her when she gets home so she can call you?"

Instead of giving her one of his cards, Troy merely said, "We'll be back." He lowered his voice just a tad, playing up to the woman's desire to be in the know. "And we'd just as soon you didn't mention our stopping by to her."

The babysitter nodded knowingly. "'Fraid she's going to run out on you? I get it. My lips are sealed." Her smugness escalated as she pantomimed placing her lips under lock and key.

Delene debated giving the older woman one of her cards. After all, she wasn't here regarding the homicide, not directly at any rate. But she knew what Cavanaugh and his partner were thinking. If alerted, Kathy/Serena might just bolt. She might just figure into Clyde's murder.

Even if she didn't, given the nature of her background, it wasn't out of the question to assume that the mother of Clyde's child wouldn't want to have anything to do with the police.

"Why don't you give me a call on my cell after she gets home?" Delene suggested, digging into her pocket and pulling out a small white card.

Just as Delene had hoped, the babysitter looked quite pleased to be included in this inner circle. Like a minor, comical character from some old grade-B movie, Louise tucked the card into her bra. Her ample bosom absorbed it, hiding all traces.

"I'll just do that," she promised.

"Think she'll call?" Kara asked as they walked away from the room less than three minutes later.

"Good chance." Delene knew that being in the middle of this little drama fed some inner need within the woman. She could remember feeling that way herself. A long time ago.

She looked at Troy as they came to the stairwell. "What do you think the odds are that she won't say anything to Kathy about you two coming around to 'talk to her' about a homicide?"

"Not so favorable," was his guess. He went down first, followed by Kara. Delene brought up the rear. "That woman was born to talk."

Delene came to the landing. The superintendent was still pushing around the already filthy mop. "That's why I tried to make her feel like she was in this with us."

He'd picked up on that. "Yeah, I noticed. Good thought." Once they were outside the building, he looked at Kara. "I'm going to get a uniform out here, have him watch the place to see if the girlfriend bolts once she gets wind that we're looking to talk to her." As he took out his cell phone to make the call, Delene began to back away. He looked in her direction. "See you later," he said, lowering his voice just a tad.

She felt something tightening inside her again. With all that was going down, she had thought that perhaps her invitation would be pushed to the side. But it wasn't. There was something different, something intimate, for lack of a better word, in his eyes when he'd said he'd see her later. It was all she could do to bank down the shiver that slid down her back.

"Right," she murmured, feeling as if her tongue were tripping over her teeth. "Seven."

"Seven," he repeated, although he was certain that

Delene didn't hear him. She was too far away. And moving fast.

Kara got into his face, the picture of curiosity. "What was that all about?"

"I don't know yet," he said quite honestly. And then he grinned at her. "But you'll be the first to find out when I do."

Kara's answer to him as she got into her car was far from G-rated. Troy tried not to laugh as he got into his own.

That evening, as she walked through the ground-floor double-glass doors leading out of the building, Delene could feel a thousand nerve endings flaring inside her. Added to that, she had that same sensation dancing through her that she'd had every time she left the house back when she had been Russell's wife.

Like someone was watching her.

Just your nerves, Dee. That's all. Nobody's watching you.

But she remained on the steps of the building, slowly scanning the area that had slipped into twilight a few minutes earlier. The parking lot was still half-full, cars belonging to people who hadn't, for one reason or another, managed to extricate themselves from their work and their desks.

Could someone be sitting in one of the vehicles now, watching her? Keeping tabs on her in order to report back to Russell?

There was no way she could be sure. She certainly

wasn't about to go running up and down the rows of cars, peering into each to see whether or not they were unoccupied.

Nobody was wasting their time, watching her. Not for any reason. She sincerely doubted that Miguel Mendoza felt angry enough to spend the man power just so she could feel unnerved.

No, one Detective Troy Cavanaugh was the reason why her imagination was running away with itself. Ever since he'd come on the scene, she really hadn't been herself.

Herself.

And just who might that be, Dee?

Just who was she these days? That scared, easily impressed young rabbit she was back then when she'd let herself be bought for a kind word, for a promise of happily-ever-after? Or was she the tough-as-nails person she was pretending to be? That's all it was, just an act. She wasn't any tougher these days than she was then. She just knew how to flip a guy twice her size now, that's all.

Well, it was a start, she told herself as she tried to bolster her self-esteem.

Thinking about what would happen later had put her off her game. She was antsy.

She needed to get this evening behind her.

Her mouth curved as she got into her car and turned on the headlights. She was dragging her feet, even though what lay ahead was all her fault.

She wondered if the miller's daughter in *Rumpel-*

stiltskin had felt the same sort of dread she did, locked up in a room full of straw and told to spin it all into gold by morning or face certain death.

Turning the wheel, she left the parking lot. She had a hunch she'd feel better about facing that task instead of the one she'd chosen for herself. Delene frowned as a song on the radio came on. Peggy Lee's classic rendition of "Fever." Not what she needed to hear tonight.

She hit a button, switching to another radio station. The second she made her choice, the music stopped registering and faded into the background.

Nobody to blame for this but yourself, Dee. You can still call it off, you know. He's not a stalker, he won't come banging on your door, saying things about you leading him on.

Do it.

She looked at the purse she'd thrown on the passenger seat. It leaned over drunkenly.

Tempting…

No, damn it, she was an adult and she'd decided to do this, to sleep with Cavanaugh, for a reason. To prove to herself that after five years, her body was just seeking reaffirmation. This was just a simple, basic urge that had crept over her, nothing more.

Just a simple sexual urge, she silently insisted. Once it was satisfied, she'd be good to go for another five years. Hopefully longer.

The glint of a headlight flashed into her rearview mirror, momentarily blinding her. Alerting her. Delene angled the mirror so that the light was no longer reflecting into her eyes.

Even as she did so, she tried to discern the make and model of the vehicle behind her. While she couldn't see if it was black or navy, she could easily discern that the car was a sedan.

An American car, she suddenly realized. She'd seen it recently in a magazine advertisement. Was the driver following her? Had he been there the whole time?

The next moment, the car made a left turn at the light. It wasn't behind her any longer.

As she drove on down the next street, Delene sighed. Relief bathed her. She was definitely getting too paranoid. She needed to get away.

Get away and do what? Spend the time worrying about Russell popping up? Better that she continue working and filling her days and nights with the myriad details that were part and parcel of her job.

And what about tonight? Just what kind of heading does that come under?

Facing your demons, Delene decided. And then she smiled again. She doubted very much if Troy Cavanaugh had ever been described by anyone, living or dead, as a demon.

It was just after six when she walked into her apartment. The light was on, just as she'd left it. After kicking off her shoes, she dropped her purse beside them.

Even though she could see almost the entire loft from where she stood at the front door, Delene went through her usual routine, first checking the locks on the windows to see if they had been tampered with.

Then she opened the top drawer in her bureau and took out the ruler she kept there. She measured the distance between the neat pile of underwear and the front of the drawer. It was a trick she'd picked up watching an old episode of a detective series on the Classic Channel.

The distance was exactly eleven inches. Just the way she'd left it. No one had been here today.

"Okay, nobody invaded your space while you were gone. What about the guy you invited to invade your space tonight?" she muttered under her breath as she shed her uniform.

Her skin insisted on tingling as she thought of the upcoming few hours.

She was doing this on her terms, her turf. That gave her the upper hand. Which, in turn, should have made her feel better.

It didn't.

Opening her closet, Delene automatically began to reach for the jeans and the baggy T-shirt she normally changed into, then stopped. She didn't want to look like something the cat had dragged in. The pride she had so carefully rebuilt and nurtured back to life these past five years dictated that she look at least a little desirable tonight.

Standing before her closet, considering her options, she chewed thoughtfully on her lower lip. There wasn't exactly a wealth of clothing to choose from.

Not like the closet she'd had when she'd been married to Russell. He'd insisted that his wife wear clothes that reflected their position in the organization. Just one of her old gowns cost more than the entire wardrobe she was looking at now.

None of the wealth had brought her happiness, she thought.

Finally she took out a very simple, very basic, black dress. She'd worn the long-sleeved dress to the last department Christmas party. And the one before that, she recalled. It was functional and just dressy enough.

"What the well-dressed woman is wearing to her own seduction tonight," Delene uttered aloud.

Once she laid out the dress on her bed, she took out a pair of black, backless four-inch heels to complete the outfit. She put the shoes by the foot of the bed, then entered the bathroom to shower and reapply her makeup.

There was a time she would have fussed with her hair, maybe wearing it up with soft tendrils framing her face. But there was really nothing to fuss with now. She looked into the mirror and shook her head.

She missed her hair.

It had been long, thick and full. Several shades darker than what it was now. Her hair had been dark blond with reddish highlights when she'd taken her vows. Everyone had remarked how she'd looked a little like a gypsy. Russell enjoyed playing with it. He had once said her hair was the first thing he'd noticed about her.

So when she'd escaped she'd cut it off until the longest part didn't even extend as far as her chin. She'd straightened what was left, then dyed it the lightest shade of blond she could find. Platinum. If anyone looked her way, she came across as just another California blonde. The last thing she wanted was to be noticeable.

But just for tonight, she wanted to feel pretty again, Delene thought as she stepped out of the bathroom and picked up the dress she'd selected. How long since she'd felt pretty? Since she'd wanted to really feel pretty? She couldn't remember that far back.

Because she was going through these motions, it wouldn't really hurt anything to go a couple of steps further. After all, she didn't want the bright young police detective with the impressive family pedigree to take one look at her, decide he could do better elsewhere and walk away.

After slipping on her dress, she zipped it up, then paused. But wasn't that the end goal? she asked herself. To do this so that they could put it behind them and never think about it again?

Delene went back into the bathroom in bare feet to run a brush through her hair. Looking at her reflection, seeing ambivalence in her eyes, she decided she was one confused woman.

Maybe she should just call this off until she got her boundaries reestablished. Better yet, maybe she should just cancel altogether. What had she been thinking, anyway?

The doorbell rang.

Too late, a little voice lamented. Or was that mocked?

Her heart went into double time.

Chapter 11

One parking space was available in guest parking when Troy pulled into Delene's garden apartment complex. Generally not superstitious, he still felt it was a favorable omen.

Taking the bottle of wine he'd brought, he made his way to her loft apartment. Somewhere in the distance, a dog howled.

He got to her apartment and rang the bell. After a couple of beats, he shifted the brown paper-bag-wrapped bottle to the other hand and rang again. Troy had no idea exactly what to expect from tonight or from the woman who had so cavalierly invited him over. The best rule of thumb when dealing with Delene D'Angelo was to expect the unexpected.

Which was fine with him. The unexpected kept him on his toes, made life interesting. Like now. He had to admit that something about the diminutive probation agent intrigued him as well as attracted him. She had managed to draw his attention more than any other woman had in a very long time.

And there was the fact that, in a way, she reminded him of his sister and his cousins. Headstrong. Stubborn. And unwilling to bend when she thought she was right. He admired the women in his family, admired their integrity and dedication. Maybe on some level, he mused as he rang a third time, they provided him with a ruler against which he measured every other female he came in contact with. And found them wanting.

When it came to women, he was spoiled. From as far back as he could remember, he'd never lacked for female companionship. All he had to do was turn around and someone was always available, willing to spend an evening, or the night, with him.

But Delene was different.

She'd made it clear that she wasn't interested in pursuing any sort of relationship that went beyond the confines of their professional worlds. Even tonight was about eliminating any obstacles to that professional interaction. Or so she said. She made it sound very, very clinical, like purging files from a computer to free up hard drive space.

Maybe he should have even been insulted. Yet that old excitement, that anticipation of exploring new ground, of being with a woman for the first time, pulsed through his veins as he stood here, in front of her apartment, ringing her doorbell.

Waiting to see her.

The chimes faded away. He'd rung three times now. She wasn't answering. Had she changed her mind? Decided that her actions would bear the kind of consequences she didn't want to deal with?

He grinned. Maybe she was nervous, though he couldn't picture her that way. The thought added to his anticipation of the evening ahead.

Troy raised his hand again, about to ring one last time when the door swung open and she was standing in the doorway. He lowered his hand, his eyes swiftly absorbing every nuance about her.

Delene's cheeks were just the slightest bit flushed, as if the temperature inside was too warm. Or her thoughts were. Her hair looked as if she'd used her fingers to comb it. On her, he thought, it looked good.

She was wearing what his sister liked to refer to as the classic little black dress. While the dress, which ended several inches above her knee, was not tight, it seemed to fall against every inviting curve she had.

No doubt about it, out of uniform Delene was a knockout, plain and simple.

Expect the unexpected. He clutched the bottle of wine a little tighter around the neck and smiled.

She could see herself reflected in his eyes. Good, she'd made the right choice, Delene thought, relaxing just a shade.

"You're not breathing," she noted.

He realized that he'd caught his breath the second he'd laid eyes on her. The moment had frozen for him. "I'm afraid if I start, you might disappear."

"If you don't start," she pointed out, "you'll black out."

He resumed breathing, but said with a smile, "Worse ways to go."

With the way he watched her, if she were an ice sculpture, she would have been reduced to tiny cubes. She tried to appear unaffected. "Is that one of your lines?"

"That's an observation," he told her, his deep voice rippling along her body. "I don't have lines."

She'd been in tight spots before. And survived. She had to remember that. The evening hadn't even begun yet and she felt like she was going under. "But you do have a reputation."

"For being honest and up front." No one could accuse him of being otherwise. He never toyed with a woman's heart. He regarded it as far too precious for that. He smiled at her. "You clean up very well, Agent D'Angelo."

His smile went straight to her gut. Worse, he was likable, damn him. She didn't want him to be likable. It was bad enough that she felt this increasingly stronger pull around him; she didn't want to have to like him, too.

Clearing her throat, Delene looked away. Anywhere but into his eyes. "Maybe for tonight you should call me Delene."

"I was hoping you'd say that." She could almost feel his eyes as they skimmed along her face. "I was also hoping you'd let me come in."

"What?" She realized that she was still standing in the doorway, her body blocking the entrance. It was as if she'd just gotten mesmerized. "Oh, right, sure." Opening the door farther, Delene stepped back, trying to deal with her embarrassment. "Come in."

Crossing the threshold, Troy handed her the bottle of wine he'd brought. He felt red was the safest choice. "This is for you."

She took it, glancing dubiously down on the telltale shape. For now, she placed it on the small table by the door, like a discarded afterthought.

"I already said we'd have sex, Cavan—" she stopped herself midname "—Troy," she said with emphasis. "You don't have to try to get me drunk."

Suspicious to the end, he thought with a slight shake of his head.

"It's a very weak wine, Delene. If you can get drunk on that, you have no tolerance for alcohol." He stared into her eyes. "And I have a deep suspicion that your tolerance is considerable."

She wasn't about to sink into those blue eyes of his. She wasn't. "Why? Because I suffer fools well?"

He was on to her. She became sharp tongued when she felt vulnerable. Something protective inside of him stirred. He wanted to chase away whatever demons haunted her.

"No, because you work so hard at being a 'tough

broad.' Holding your liquor just goes with the image."
He appraised her for a long moment, deliberately
stretching it out. She was softer tonight, more femi-
nine despite the so-called "point" of the evening. His
voice softened just a little as he burrowed into her personal space. "Someone threaten your boundaries before, Delene?"

Her eyes narrowed ever so slightly. "No personal
questions."

Yes, he was definitely beginning to see through her.
"Are there ground rules for tonight?"

Damn it, Cavanaugh was pushing his way into her
space. And now she wasn't quite as sure about all this
as she'd been even thirty minutes ago, when she'd
begun to doubt the wisdom of her actions.

Delene scrambled to reestablish the boundaries
around her. "There are ground rules for everything."

He cupped her face in his hands as an excitement
began to mount within him. He heard her catch her
breath. His excitement heightened further still. "Maybe
you'd better go over them," he coaxed.

How could she suddenly feel as if she was short of
breath? They hadn't done anything yet. Yet it seemed
difficult to drag sufficient air into her lungs. Worse,
her head began to spin.

The moment his lips whispered along her cheek,
Delene swore she could feel something begin to dissolve inside her.

It took everything she had not to melt into him. She
clenched her hands at her sides. "There's no need for

foreplay," she told him, trying desperately to sound unaffected.

"There's always a need for foreplay."

His breath skimmed along her skin as he answered. Anticipation roared through her veins.

Idiot, what were you thinking? she mocked herself.

She had not been with a man in five years. Russell had been her first lover. Her only lover. Lovemaking, sex—all that was an episode of her life she'd thought she was through with when she'd escaped and dissolved her nightmare of a marriage. When she'd put forth her invitation to Troy, she'd been certain that she could go through this with nothing more than a physical reaction. But now she was no longer so certain. Not certain at all.

Because strange things were going on inside of her. Cleaving to what he was doing. Rallying and cheering. And wanting more. So much more.

But she was nothing if not a fighter. Willing her hands to remain still at her side, she murmured, "You're trying to seduce me."

He raised his head from the tender hollow of her throat to look at her. The expression in his eyes was wickedly delicious. She felt herself melting a little more.

"How'm I doing?" he asked softly.

Spectacularly.

The single-word response throbbed through her brain. Her hands had mutinied against her. She realized that she was holding on to his arms now. Just when had that happened?

Probably when she felt her knees giving out. "You don't have to do this." She forced the words out with effort. "I already said I'd have sex with you."

Troy laid a finger to her lips, his eyes on hers. If she didn't know better, she would have said where he'd touched had just burst into flame. "Shh. I like doing things my own way."

Desperation rose another notch inside her. Damn it, she'd wanted to have sex with him, to discharge whatever was humming inside of her. What he was doing wasn't discharging her urge. He was fanning the flames, making them stretch and grow so that she was in danger of burning up.

Things were happening inside of her, scrambling for high ground as wide, all-encompassing want and need continued to grow, threatened to obliterate her.

He was taking the last shred of control away for her. Any second now, she was going to be on the floor, a puddle of submission.

The very *last* thing she wanted.

Never again did she want to hand control over her to a man. This had to stop. *Had to.*

The woman in his arms seemed to snap to attention. He could have sworn he'd heard her telepathically communicate the word *Geronimo,* forwarding it to his brain.

The next moment, she'd wrapped her arms around his neck and pressed her lips against his.

Hard.

He hadn't planned on kissing her mouth, yet. He

had wanted to work his way up to it, setting the stage for the pleasurable encounter because he believed that making love to a woman wasn't just the interlocking of sexual organs. That was too easy. You could make love to a woman with your eyes, with your hands, with every fiber of your being. Which was exactly what he had intended on doing with Delene.

But Delene had broadsided him. She had caused a power surge inside of him that came out of left field and in its wake had left him shaken and wanting. Not to mention scorched.

Desire for this woman had existed from the very first, but he'd just assumed he could manage it, enjoy and act upon it when he chose the moment. But suddenly, when she'd kissed him with feeling, the mental blueprints he'd laid out had gone up in flames. Instead, he found himself in the grip of something that took his very breath away, an occurrence that had never happened.

That excited him beyond description.

It was as if he'd gotten his foot caught in the stirrup of a galloping horse. He couldn't even run to keep up.

So, in a last-ditch effort to regain control, Troy said the first thing that popped into his mind. "Whoa, take it easy." He drew his head back. His hands lightly gripped her shoulders to keep her in place. "We have all night."

No, no they didn't, she thought urgently. She didn't. *She* had to get in front of this before it ran her down and left her flatter than the long white dividing line on the highway. He was sweeping her away, out to sea without a twig to hang on to, and she had to stop it, had to be the one in charge. If she wasn't, she had this awful feeling she was doomed.

The problem was, the more she tried to take control, the more quickly she lost it, because what she attempted to do to him was backfiring and taking her along for the ride.

The more she kissed Troy, the more she wanted to kiss him. The more she wanted him to kiss her. To take her. The more she wanted to grab on to this feeling that coursed through her veins, making her insane. It was like stumbling upon a ravenous hunger. A hunger that threatened to have her go up in smoke if she didn't satiate it.

He couldn't recognize himself, didn't want to waste the time trying. All he knew was that Delene had unleashed myriad intense sensations through him, intense sensations he was determined to enjoy. And to introduce her to.

Her fingers scrambled over his body, tugging at his shirt, tearing the buttons from the holes that kept them in place. The moment she was finished, he flung his shirt off, even as he began to feel for the zipper at the back of her dress. Finding it, he quickly pulled it down to its base.

Her dress fell from her body like a sigh.

Or maybe the sigh came from him. Again, there was no time to wonder, only time to act.

He felt—rather than saw—the delicate lingerie she had on. The soft, silken texture complemented the silken skin he discovered beneath. He had to hold himself in check not to rip the garments from her. The desire for speed, for urgency, was something new. A first.

The thought occurred to him distantly, because not even his first time had been fueled with this kind of energy, this kind of desire.

He coaxed the material from her body and sensed her heat even as she shivered against him, nude. Her fingers still frantically worked away at the remainder of his clothing, tugging on his belt. A frustrated sound echoed against his mouth.

Troy struggled to keep his smile from emerging, knowing she'd think he was laughing at her when nothing was further from the truth. Delight was responsible for the amused expression attempting even now to surface.

Stilling the fingers that were making him quiver with anticipation, Troy undid his belt for her, was about to pull the short zipper down when he felt her hands usurping his. Felt her fingertips moving the metal teeth apart little by little.

Felt her touching him through the layers that still remained between them. He was ready for her.

She'd wrenched control from his hands. But for Troy, it wasn't about control, had never been about control. But it *had* turned into a matter of not getting swept away in the undertow.

Urgently she pressed her body against his. An indistinguishable sound escaped her lips as she savored the heat traveling up and down every inch of her, exuding from every pore of her body. And from his.

Delene stifled a cry as he swept his hands over her, caressing her body softly. Possessively. She twisted and turned against him, wanting him inside of her. Wanting to reach the climax that now seemed like almost a dream to her.

It had been five years.

Five long years. At the touch of his clever hands, hands that seemed to prime her at every pass, her body had slipped out of its coma. It left her now with an insatiable need to feel the surge, the thrill of lovemaking. She felt him hard against her. Felt his heat transferring itself to her. Felt his fingers opening the clasp at her back.

The black bra she'd chosen so carefully only a short while ago was now on the floor, beside her dress. Beside her sanity.

Slick and damp, desperate for a release, she felt herself being lifted into the air, then deposited on her bed. Somehow his lips never left hers, never broke contact. He was over her, blocking out the rest of the world. She didn't care. She arched against him.

Ready. Waiting.

But rather than take her, rather than enter and for a moment lose himself within her, Troy gathered her to him and continued kissing her. Stealing the very air from her lungs.

Just when she was certain she wasn't going to breathe again, his lips left hers, traveling along her damp skin, setting every inch of her on fire each place they touched.

She could hear him breathing. He was as short of breath as she was. Somehow that was comforting. But not nearly as comforting as having him.

As being one with him.

Delene tried to reach for him, but instead of being able to draw Troy up, he'd moved lower along her body, slowly forging a path down to her core as she wriggled beneath him.

With short, staccato movements, his tongue dampened the hollow of her belly. And then, suddenly, there were explosions going off in her veins. Reaching the very center of her sexuality, Troy brought her blood up to almost its boiling point. Moaning, saying things she couldn't even repeat, she felt his tongue caressing her in ways that Russell had never even attempted.

And wild sparks consumed her until she tottered on the very brink of exhaustion. Wanting more. Afraid that if there was more, she wouldn't be able to gather herself back up again.

Depleted, her lungs ached. She was almost unable to draw in a breath as she felt Troy finally slide his body up over her.

The quickening in her loins surprised her. The way he gently framed her face again even more so.

"Open your eyes for me, Delene." At first she thought she imagined the words, but then she knew he was saying them to her. Only then did she realize that her eyes had been squeezed shut this whole time.

Squeezed shut as the whirlpool sucked her deeper into its vortex.

When she did as he asked, she expected to see that same look she'd seen on Russell's face. The one that fairly crowed with superiority. The one that said he literally owned her.

Instead she saw something akin to awed tenderness in Troy's eyes. A lump materialized in her throat.

He linked his hands with hers, as if they were one in this.

Troy had no need to move her legs apart, she was waiting for him. Ready and so eager, it was beyond her ability to reason it out.

"Now," she cried as pulses throbbed through her, begging for one last release. One last surge. "Now."

His smile went straight to the heart of her, even as she desperately tried to deflect it. "I never argue with a lady."

Troy slipped into her. Not plunged the way Russell had, as if it were an attack, as if he needed one more way to establish his dominance over her, but slipped inside gently. He began the rhythmic dance slowly and only stepped up the tempo with each pass.

But when she began to move feverishly against him, all thoughts of a slow progression were cast aside. He had no choice but to hurry to keep up. Because he didn't want her reaching the summit without him.

She didn't.

They came there together.

Chapter 12

Troy kept his hands linked with hers a moment longer, absorbing the warmth of her body, letting it mingle with his. The euphoria slowly slipped away as the world drew back into focus. He could still feel his heart pounding against hers, as if they'd both just run to the limit of their endurance.

His breathing was as erratic as hers. He could feel her breath along his cheek, could feel something stirring, ever so distantly, inside him.

Again.

He would have smiled if he'd had the energy, but she'd completely depleted him of it. When he finally shifted his body from hers, Troy gathered Delene to him.

She tried to pull her thoughts back into focus, to pull herself out of the swirling cauldron of emotions that overwhelmed her.

So much ground to regain.

Her space had been breached as surely as if it had been a balloon speared by a javelin. How did she begin to reestablish her boundaries? She didn't know, but she had to. Survival depended on it.

He encased her in his arms. She struggled to break free, her eyes on his. "What are you doing?"

Troy raised an eyebrow at the question. He would have thought the answer was self-explanatory, but then nothing with Delene ever seemed to be as cut-and-dried as it appeared.

"Holding you." It came out partially as a question, as he found himself waiting for her to put another interpretation on it. She was suddenly stiff as a board. As if she was ready to block and deflect whatever came her way.

Russell had never held her, never attempted to do anything except either roll over and go to sleep or get up and go about his business, the lovemaking between them carrying no more significance to him than shining his shoes. Cavanaugh's answer raised her suspicions as she searched for an ulterior motive.

"Why?"

He felt as if he was under interrogation. Because he was laid-back, he let her tone slide. "I don't know. I thought it was kind of nice."

"For me." Was this pity on his part? Or part of a plan to undermine her? She hated feeling like this—it ruined the moment. But better a ruined moment than facing something of more dire consequences.

"Hopefully for you," Troy allowed, then smiled. "Definitely for me." Because there was no response to his teasing answer, he raised himself on his elbow and looked down at her. "What's the matter, Delene, did I do something wrong?"

Yes, you made me feel things again. I'm not supposed to feel things. I'm not supposed to feel anything.

But in the absolute sense, no, he hadn't done anything wrong. He'd done everything right. Perfect. He'd made love to her just the way a woman would have wanted to be made love to. As if she mattered.

Suspicion clouded her eyes as she looked at him. "What are you after?"

"After?" he repeated. "You mean like a compliment or a gold star?"

She dug her elbow into the mattress, attempting to sit up. But his body blocked her way. Confining her. She pushed him back and faced him. "No, I mean what are you after? Why did you make love like that?"

Okay, now she'd really lost him, Troy thought. "Like what?"

"Like I mattered," she cried in frustration. Why was he toying with her this way? "Like this mattered." She gestured around at the bed and them.

He took a moment before answering, knowing if he spoke immediately she'd accuse him of pandering to her. If he were in the habit, she would be the last person he would pander to. She was the kind who respected and needed complete honesty.

"Maybe because it did. It does."

A dismissive laugh escaped her lips. "We hardly know each other."

Time didn't have all that much to do with it. "Some people live a lifetime next to one another and don't know each other at all. For others, it takes only a day." Before she could scoff, he said, "My father proposed to my mother on their first date. They were married for twenty-five years."

"Before they got divorced?" she guessed.

"No," Troy corrected. "Before my mother died."

The stark, solitary statement pierced the armor Delene was trying to cover herself with. "Oh. I'm sorry."

It had been more than five years ago and he still missed her terribly, as did his siblings. "We all are." Troy thought of how lost his father had seemed at his mother's funeral. It was the first time he'd ever realized that his father wasn't larger-than-life. "Most of all, my father."

She'd forgotten whose son he was. "That would be the chief of detectives, Brian Cavanaugh?"

Troy smiled. He couldn't remember a day he hadn't been proud of his father, even while he was rebelling against the man's authority when he was a teenager. "The very same."

"So are you planning on proposing to me now?" Delene asked dryly.

She watched as the smile crinkled his eyes. "I like

keeping my options open." Shifting, he drew a sheet over them. Without the heat of lovemaking, the loft felt a little chilled. "Besides, we haven't had a first date yet."

Something impossibly sweet blossomed within her when he'd covered them both. She felt like she was struggling madly to stay afloat instead of going under for the third time. "What's this called?"

To him a date meant going out. Meant picking a woman up and enjoying her company while doing something with her. This was just "dropping over."

Troy pretended to give her question a moment's thought. "To the best of my understanding, a command performance." Lowering his head, he pressed a kiss first to her temple, then her cheek. Excitement, fueled by desire, built inside him. Damn, but he wanted her again. It was as if what had just happened was an appetizer and he was anticipating the main course. "The nice thing about command performances," he told her, each word lingering on her skin as he continued kissing her softly, "is that you get to do curtain calls—and encores."

He was making coherent thought increasingly difficult for her. Her body was priming itself for him again. "Encores?"

He tugged away a little of the sheet he'd just covered her with, exposing a breast. He caressed it even as he brought his mouth down over the tip. Feeling her move against him just created more excitement within him.

"You know, a little bit of the performance." He raised his head, a mischievous smile gracing his lips as he looked at her. "Or in some cases, a whole new number."

Her limbs felt leaden as desire poured itself through her veins. "You're ready to do this again?" she asked incredulously.

His look was impossibly sexy. "I am if you are." His hand moved over her, not possessively, but like a tourist making a particularly pleasing pilgrimage. "It wouldn't be half the fun if you weren't there."

Her head spun once more. She struggled to make sense of his words. "So you're asking me if I want to?"

His answer was in her eyes. Desire as bold, as consuming as his. But he knew better than to assume anything. Despite her bravado, the lady needed kid-glove treatment.

"Yes," he breathed just before his mouth covered hers.

Delene's eyes fluttered shut as he kissed her. As he took all control out of her hands again.

But this time she realized she wasn't holding on to the reins so tightly. Wasn't getting rope burns across her palms as she tried to keep them from slipping away.

"Well, since you're already here..." Her voice trailed off.

He chuckled, his breath tickling her neck. "My sentiments exactly."

And then there was no room for words. No room for anything except the sensations that crescendoed through both of them.

* * *

Troy made love to her twice more that night. When heaven and earth shifted positions the second time, she was far too exhausted to form a complete thought. Delene fell asleep in his arms, too tired to move, too tired even to contemplate resurrecting the barriers that had fallen beneath the onslaught of his lips.

A moment before she sank into oblivion, entertaining thoughts that maybe, just maybe, she was entitled to some small shred of happiness after all, the door to her loft flew open. It banged against the opposite wall before it was closed again.

Terror leaped into her throat.

He'd found her.

Russell was standing at the foot of her bed, a gun in his hand.

Oh, God, why had she forgotten to put her weapon under the pillow the way she did each night? Why this one time when she needed it most?

He was as tall, as dark, as handsome as she remembered. And as demonic. His dark blue eyes blazed holes into her. "You bitch! You worthless little whore! I always knew that when I'd find you, you'd be in bed with some bastard!"

The gun. Where was her gun? Where had she left it? Delene frantically scanned the room, her mind a blank.

"We're divorced," she cried, knowing it was useless to try to reason with him. Somehow she had to distract him. There were two of them; Troy would save her.

But who would save Troy? She knew what Russell was capable of.

"I don't belong to you anymore!" She felt, more than saw, Troy sitting up in the bed. She should have never let him come here, never invited him. If anything happened to him because of her, she'd never forgive herself.

The malevolence exuding from Russell seemed to grow like a force of nature, darkening the room. He sneered contemptuously at her. "You'll always belong to me."

"Hey, buddy," Troy called to him so calmly, Delene realized he didn't understand just how serious the situation was. "I think you'd better leave."

The sneer on Russell's face turned almost evil as he shifted his attention to Troy. "Do you, now? Well, I think I should stay. But you, you're the one who's leaving. Now."

Faster than a heartbeat, he aimed the gun he was holding point-blank at Troy.

"No, Russell! No!" Delene cried.

Russell fired before she could throw herself in front of Troy.

Troy's blood began to pool all around her on the bed, seeping into the sheets, into the mattress. Into her. Filled with horror, with a bottomless sense of dread and loss, Delene started screaming.

Cursing her as he grabbed her by the arms, Russell pulled her from the bed and began to shake her.

"You're mine, do you hear me? Mine. I'll see you

six feet in the ground before I ever, *ever* let you go. Do you hear me?"

Everything fell apart around her. There was blood everywhere, on the very walls. Delene couldn't stop screaming. She clawed at Russell, trying to hurt him, wishing she could rip his heart out the way he'd just ripped out hers.

"Delene, stop it! Delene, it's all right," Russell shouted over her screams. "You're safe, do you understand? You're safe. Stop screaming." As he repeated the refrain over and over again, his voice began to change.

She could have sworn he sounded just like Troy. But that was impossible. Troy was dead. Russell had just killed him.

And he was going to kill her next; she just knew it.

And still he repeated in Troy's voice, "It's all right. It's all right."

When he tried to hold her to him, she resisted with all her might. But he didn't smell like Russell. Didn't have on the high-end cologne that Russell liked to import.

The clean and rugged scent slowly began to penetrate her brain.

Troy.

Those were his arms holding her fast. His lips against her hair. His voice telling her it was all right.

Shaken, Delene realized she was still in her loft. Still in the bed. A second later her eyes flew open. It *was* Troy.

He was alive!

The words beat frantically in her breast. He was alive! She began to scramble from the bed. "We have to get you to the hospital. Quick!"

"Hospital?" he echoed dumbfoundingly. "What are you talking about?"

But she was staring at the sheets, her eyes wide with disbelief. Everything had been red a moment ago. "Blood." She looked up at him, her fingers feathering gingerly along his chest. Where the bullet hole had been. Where it no longer was. "Where's the blood?"

So, he'd made his way into her subconscious. But not in a good way. "Safely in my veins. What kind of a dream did you just have?"

It wasn't real. None of it. She'd dreamed it all. Russell wasn't here.

Relieved, suddenly unspeakably exhausted, Delene slumped against Troy. "A dream," she repeated. She drew in a long breath before saying, "A nightmare. Just a nightmare."

His ears were still ringing from her screams. She'd come close to giving him heart failure. One moment they were asleep, the next she was screaming in his ear, beating him with her fists. He wanted to know more. "It wasn't 'just' a nightmare, not for you to have that kind of a reaction."

She drew away from him. And into herself. Sitting up, she hugged her knees to her.

It was just a nightmare. Russell hasn't found me. Hasn't killed Troy.

Getting her bearings, Delene dragged her hand

through her hair. "I get them sometimes. Nightmares," she repeated, then shrugged. "Sorry, didn't mean to scare you."

He wasn't thinking about himself right now. Troy gazed at her intently. "Who's Russell?" Whoever he was, the man figured heavily into her life and he wanted to know how.

Her head jerked up and she stared at him. How did he know about Russell? "What?"

"Russell," Troy repeated, enunciating the name slowly. He prodded her memory. "You were pleading with him."

Delene stared straight ahead into the shadows within the loft as she shook her head. "Don't remember. Just a name."

"I think you do remember. Talk it out, Delene."

Anger joined hands with defensiveness. She looked at him belligerently. "What are you, my shrink now?"

"No," he said evenly, although it bothered him that Delene would lie to him like this. "I'm just a willing pair of ears. You're still shaking," he pointed out.

"Just the aftermath of lovemaking," she retorted flippantly.

The hell it was. Why was she keeping him out? "Look, you were screaming and crying, and from the look on your face, it obviously isn't the first time. Now, who's Russell?"

The biggest mistake of my life. But she held her ground, shaking her head. "You don't want to know."

Now she *really* had his curiosity piqued. "If I didn't, I wouldn't have asked."

No, she supposed he wouldn't have. She wrapped her arms around herself, cold down to the bone. "Maybe I don't want to tell you."

Now that he could believe. But in believing it, something hurt inside. "What just happened here isn't about sex, Delene, it's about intimacy. Intimacy can't happen if you don't trust someone."

She raised her chin. The dream had been an omen. An omen telling her that she was playing with fire, making love with another man. If Russell ever *did* find out, Troy's life would be over. It was time to end this before it became any more involved.

"Maybe I don't want intimacy."

He didn't believe that. Not the way she'd made love with him. There was a vulnerable woman beneath the trappings. "It's not about what you want, it's about what you need."

There he went again, presuming to know what went on inside of her head. "What I don't need is someone playing psychiatrist on me."

She wasn't going to talk to him. He'd seen stubbornness like this before. Up close and personal in his own family. The only way to proceed was to wait this out.

Troy got out of bed, completely oblivious to the fact that he was stark naked. "Okay. Well, you know where to find me if you change your mind."

She tried not to stare. It wasn't easy. But the nervous flutter in her veins helped redirect her attention to a degree. "What are you doing?"

"Getting my things together." He picked up his jeans and shirt as he looked around for his shoes.

A panic rose from nowhere, skittering through her. She didn't want to be alone. "You're leaving?"

He turned to face her, his arms full of his clothes. "Well, you made it pretty clear that you don't want me to stay."

Delene didn't answer. She sat in silence as he got dressed. Told herself that she didn't need to talk, didn't need to play out some so-called fantasy humming in his brain, making him out to be the kindly instrument of her salvation.

And she had almost managed to convince herself.

Until he had his hand on the doorknob.

She shut her eyes. *Just a few seconds more.* If she could just hang on a few seconds longer, he'd be out the door.

And she'd be alone.

As alone as she'd been before she'd invited him over.

Troy opened the door.

"He's my husband."

Very slowly Troy turned from the door. Finally. It took her long enough. If he'd walked any slower, he would have been moving backward. He looked at her.

"Husband?" he repeated. There was no wedding ring on her finger. Men were divided as to whether or not they wore a symbol of their marriage, but most women he knew did so proudly.

"Ex-husband," she clarified, "thanks to a Mexican decree." She knew all the words Russell would have used once the papers had arrived. He would have wanted to kill the mail carrier. "He doesn't recognize it," she added. "As a lawyer, I figure he's probably looked into ways to get around it."

Troy didn't care about the man's profession, he cared about the way she looked when she'd thought the man was here. Terrified. "Did he beat you?"

She stiffened. Only pathetic weaklings let themselves be beaten. Was that what Troy thought of her? "What makes you ask that?"

There was no judgment in his voice. "I've been a cop for a while, Delene." He sat down on her bed. "You get to know the signs."

She shrugged, distancing herself from the memories. Or trying to.

"Yes, he beat me. But not before he sucked out my soul." She sighed. She'd started this. Maybe Cavanaugh had a right to know. So he'd see why he couldn't continue any kind of a personal relationship with her. My God, she was thinking relationships. She really *was* shaken up. "He's a successful lawyer for the Palladino family in Colorado and he doesn't believe in taking no for an answer."

Glancing at Troy, she could see he wanted more. She gave it to him. "I met Russell when I was nineteen. He was everything I thought I wanted. Tall, dark, handsome, rich—and he was charming." She rolled her eyes, remembering. God, she'd been so dumb then. "Oh so charming. And he wanted me. Every woman at every gathering we ever went to looked at me with envy, wishing they were in my place."

She sighed. "After a while, I wished one of them had been. So I could get free." But she was free now, she reminded herself. And she'd die before she gave that up. "He swept me off my feet, asked me to marry him after we'd been together two months. Said I made him happy."

She turned to face him. "My father, as you figured out the other day, deserted my mother and me when I was very young. My mother, as you also guessed, kind of disintegrated little by little, and I was pretty much on my own by the time I graduated from high school. When this man—who could have anyone— wanted me, I was beside myself with joy at how lucky I had finally become."

Her mouth quirked. *Stupid, stupid.* "I guess that comes under the heading of be careful what you wish for."

He didn't want her putting blame on herself. "What made him finally let you go?"

She laughed. That was funny. Russell never released anything he owned. "He didn't. He beat me within an inch of my life for trying to get away. I landed in the hospital on life support, so badly beaten, the plastic surgeon who worked on my face told me he'd used up his lifetime supply of miracles putting me back together again."

She saw a flash of anger in Troy's eyes. Her first instinct was that it was directed against her, against her stupidity for being with a man like Russell. But then she realized that Troy was angry at Russell.

The thought left her in awe. "I knew that if I went home with Russell, the next time he thought I had committed some minor infringement, he'd kill me. So the second I had any strength at all, I bribed an orderly. He helped smuggle me out of the hospital in the middle of the night." Her mouth curved. Her story sounded so melodramatic, but every word was true. "I cut and dyed my hair, changed my name and I've never looked back since."

She'd left out one detail. "What about your mother?"

Delene shook her head. There was nothing there to draw her back. "My mother was on his side. She was the one who told him that I was getting ready to leave him again—"

"Again?"

She nodded. "I'd tried once before, unsuccessfully. He'd beat me then, too, but not as badly as he did this time." The smile on her lips had no trace of humor in it. "My mother thought Russell was a great catch for me."

He looked at her for a long moment, absorbing what she'd told him, trying desperately to keep the anger raging through his veins from spilling out. She'd said she'd changed her name. That would explain why there was no trace of Delene D'Angelo older than five years. "What's your real name?"

Delene pressed her lips together. "The person I was

is dead. I'm Delene D'Angelo. That's all you need to know."

He nodded. "All right."

His response stunned her. "You're not going to press me?" she asked in disbelief. "You're all right with not knowing?"

When she was ready, she'd tell him. He didn't want her thinking of him as being in the same category as her ex. "I know you as Delene. That's all that I need. I was just curious." Because she looked so vulnerable, so fragile, he couldn't help himself. He took her into his arms.

Delene saw the long, angry scratch on his arm. "I did that?"

"Yeah."

She twisted from his arms, wanting to get to the medicine cabinet. "Let me put something on it before it becomes infected."

Troy pulled her to him. She was being maternal, but he didn't need a mother right now. "Later. Right now I just need to hold you."

She saw through his words. "You mean you think I need to be held."

He laughed, shaking his head. "You, me, what difference does it make? This isn't a debate, Delene. It's just a hug. For both of us," he amended in order to please her.

She settled back in his arms, telling herself it was a mistake to feel so comfortable.

She stayed where she was, anyway.

Chapter 13

The ringing sound penetrated her brain in layers, but failed to identify its source. Eyes still shut, convinced she'd been asleep only five minutes, six at the utmost, Delene felt around on the nightstand for her alarm clock. Hitting it once did nothing to still the ringing.

Neither did groping for the telephone beside it.

Trying desperately to get her mind to surface, still in the throes of a deep sleep, she held the receiver against her ear.

"Hello? Hello?" she demanded between long, deep breaths. Only the dial tone droned in response.

"I think it's your cell phone," the voice beside her said.

Delene jerked awake with a start, her eyes flying

open and widening as she stared at the man lying beside her in the bed.

The naked man lying beside her in the bed.

A low-key, sexy smile slipped across Troy's lips in response to her scrutiny. "Sorry, didn't mean to startle you."

Reaching over her, he plucked the small, silver cell phone from the edge of the nightstand and handed it to her. The experience was more than fleetingly pleasurable, at least for him, he thought. She looked as if she was having trouble digesting his presence.

"Troy Cavanaugh." He pretended to introduce himself. "The man you slept with last night, quite spectacularly, I might add."

Delene blew out a breath, mentally scrambling to get her bearings. Last night and early this morning came back to her like a pony express rider on the first leg of his journey.

She cleared her throat and prayed she sounded less rattled than she felt. "I know who you are, I'm just not used to waking up with someone in my bed."

That can change, Troy thought. He decided that maybe it was best to keep the response silent for the time being. Especially since he wasn't altogether sure just what to do with this morning-after feeling.

Something deeper was happening to him. Something had occurred last night, something beyond just the friendly, if somewhat intense, coupling of two people who enjoyed each other's company.

This was going to have consequences.

Whether he wanted to welcome those consequences, to embrace them, or to vacate the premises with no forwarding address, he hadn't quite worked out yet. All these years, he'd liked being free, being him. He'd glimpsed a new "him" last night, felt like a slightly different version of himself at this predawn hour, and that was going to take some analyzing.

Sitting up, he moved the hair away from her neck and pressed a kiss there. She squirmed and waved her hand at him, indicating that she wanted him to move back.

Indicating that he was interfering with her ability to think. He liked that. Because she sure as hell had interfered with his.

Clutching the small phone in her hand, Delene pressed it to her ear. "Hello?"

"She's here," a woman's voice rasped.

It took Delene less than a moment to realize who was on the other end of the line and who the "she" was that the woman was referring to. If there was an ounce of sleep left within her, it was gone now. "Kathy Springer?" Beside her, she felt Troy stiffen. He'd stopped trying to assault her ramparts, thank God.

"I don't know any Kathy," Louise Patton insisted, impatience and annoyance resonating in her voice, "but Serena Sherman's in the next room and she's packing."

Delene kicked the sheet aside. She had to get moving. "I'm on my way. Thank you."

"Talk is cheap." It was clear that the other woman was waiting for something.

"You'll be compensated," Delene promised. She swung her legs out of the bed. "Keep her there as long as you can."

It was hard for Troy to focus on what he'd just pieced together from Delene's side of the conversation. She got up, utterly nude with the last strains of moonlight playing over her more-than-perfect body.

Somehow he managed to find his voice. "That the babysitter?"

Delene crossed over to the bureau. She nodded as she grabbed fresh undergarments from a middle drawer. "She says Kathy's packing. I asked her to stall as long as possible."

Despite his dedication, he could feel his body priming. Wanting her. Work had always come first. This was a new experience.

He got out on his side and began to locate his clothes which had somehow gotten scattered. "You should have told her to tie the woman up. That way we'd have a little extra time."

She glanced at him as she hooked her bra, then stepped into her underwear. "I can get dressed fast," she told him, thinking he might be one of those men who thought all women took a minimum of an hour to get ready.

"I wasn't thinking about you getting dressed." Looking at her, he tugged on his own jeans. "I was thinking about another encore."

Pushing her closet door open, she decided to forgo putting on a uniform just yet. Instead, she took out a sweater and jeans. "You keep on doing encores and the show might have to close early."

Mischief and something more glinted in his eyes as he watched her from the foot of the bed. "But it would have had a hell of a run before that."

Delene laughed. It felt good. When was the last time she'd actually laughed out loud? She couldn't remember. Couldn't recall being happy enough to even feel like laughing.

Careful, a voice inside her warned. *Don't get carried away.*

She glanced at her watch as she slipped on her shoes. "Speaking of running—"

"Gotcha." Dressed, Troy looked around for his footwear. He'd located one shoe, but the second one was eluding him. It hadn't been beneath his clothes. He moved aside her dress on the floor, putting it on the bed. No shoe.

Getting down on all fours, he looked under the bed and saw that somehow his left shoe had gotten kicked underneath. Out of reach, no matter which way he moved, he had to take his other shoe and use the tip to coax out the errant loafer.

By the time he put it on, Delene was dressed and running her fingers through her hair in lieu of a comb. He shook his head in admiration. "Damn, you *are* fast."

She was already at the door. And smiling. "Just where it counts."

He had no idea what that meant, but he knew he wanted to explore it further as soon as they had time.

"We'll go in my car," he said to the back of her head as they hurried down the stone stairs.

The only light came from the moon and a tall lamp left on by the city. The residents in the surrounding apartments were all still asleep.

Already halfway to her carport, Delene stopped to look at him. "Why your car?"

If he noticed that she was challenging him, as if this was a control issue, he deliberately didn't show it. "Because my car has the dispatch radio," he told her easily.

Torn, she hesitated for a moment longer. "We can use both."

He unlocked his door. "One's faster."

She surrendered, although she wasn't quite certain why. With a snort, she crossed to his vehicle and got into the passenger side. "That makes no sense."

Troy turned the ignition on. "Humor me."

Delene slid the seat belt's metal tongue into the appropriate slot. "I thought that was what last night was about."

It was his turn to laugh. Deeply. The sound burrowed its way into her belly, warming her.

Careful, Dee, she warned herself again. *You don't want to get used to this.*

But the problem was, part of her *did* want to get used to this. Did want to feel at ease with a man. Especially a man who had so successfully moved the earth beneath her feet with his lovemaking.

"We'll discuss that later," he told her, turning his car around. They were on the main road in a matter of seconds. Except for two other vehicles, theirs was the only car traveling north.

She stared at his profile. Light from passing street lamps moved in and out of the vehicle, highlighting the interior and then casting it back into semidarkness. Was he putting her on? Or was that a promise of some sort? "Later? There's going to be a later?"

He glanced at her before looking back at the road. "Has to be. Because there can't be a now." And he really wanted to make slow, languid love to her again. "We've got a witness to question."

She detected something in his voice, something beyond the latent desire. "You think she did it, don't you?"

He inclined his head slightly. "Packing up in the middle of the night kind of points in that direction."

Delene tried to make excuses for the woman she'd never met. "Maybe she's trying to get away from Mendoza's men. Maybe she saw something."

"Maybe," he allowed. Anything was possible, but somehow he doubted it. Troy spared a glance at the woman whose appetite for lovemaking had turned out to be a match for his own. "Since when do you have optimistic thoughts?"

Delene retreated. "Optimistic?" she scoffed.

You're not quite pulling this off, Delene, he thought, amused. "I thought this job made you see the worst in everyone."

It wasn't the job that had tainted her view of humanity. "I saw the worst long before I came to work for the probation department."

Since she seemed to be in a somewhat talkative mood, he decided to ask her another question that was bothering him. "Why did you come to work in the department?"

She shifted in her seat, impatient to be there already. Afraid that somehow Kathy would bolt and they wouldn't be able to find her.

"So I could stay on top of the drug dealers." She looked at him to see how he took her answer. The expression on his face told her it wasn't the reply he'd expected. "For every drug dealer who gets busted and sent away, there's that much less revenue being generated for Russell's 'clients.'"

She knew that there were a great many dealers and sources of drugs, but somehow she felt that this all tied in with the people Russell represented. She could *feel* it.

Given what she'd told him, he would have thought she'd want to maintain a low profile. "Most people would just try to keep clear of that."

She shrugged, looking forward. Willing time to stand still and the distance to disappear. "Yeah well, I'm not like most people."

Now there was an understatement, he thought.

"Point taken," Troy acknowledged.

Taking the receiver from his radio, he put in a call to the policeman he'd left posted, watching the apartment building Kathy Springer lived in. If the babysitter failed to keep Kathy distracted long enough for them to arrive, it was up to the patrolman.

* * *

Jagged, half-chewed nails caught in Kathy Springer's stringy, dirty-blond hair as she ran her thin fingers through it nervously. Standing just a few feet away from the broken-down vehicle in which she was planning to make her escape, she looked at the policeman who had suddenly gotten in her way.

"I haven't done anything," she cried, trying to push past him. It was like a twig trying to push down a tree. "Get out of my way."

The little girl, a tiny carbon copy of her mother, was holding on to Kathy's short skirt. The child was wailing, frightened by all the noise and the tall, thin policeman looming over her mother.

They could hear Rachel crying and Kathy pleading as they pulled up into the parking lot.

They'd gotten here just in time, Delene thought. "Looks like the first line of defense failed," she observed just before she jumped out of Troy's boat of a car.

Was she crazy? "You're supposed to wait until the car comes to a full stop," Troy cried as he pulled up the hand brake. He left the vehicle double parked behind a vintage VW Bug and he ran after Delene.

Kathy Springer was breathing hard. Her mascara had long since smudged, giving her the appearance of a raccoon. A terrified raccoon, now that two more officials approached. Clearly panicked, she seemed to search for somewhere to run, an avenue of escape left open to her.

There was none.

And just like that, Kathy Springer surrendered. Her thin shoulders slumped in abject defeat.

"Kathy Springer?" Troy called out to her.

There was little light in her eyes as she looked in his direction. "Yeah."

Troy took out his badge and held it out for her as he approached. "I'm Detective Cavanaugh." Putting his badge away, he nodded at Delene. "This is Probation Agent D'Angelo. We'd like a few words with you."

Still distrustful as well as nervous, Kathy wrinkled up her brow. "You want to talk? Just talk?"

Troy glanced at Delene before answering. Given how she felt about control, he was surprised that she was letting him take the lead. "Yes. Why don't we go back upstairs to your apartment?"

But Kathy seemed disinclined to give up any ground. "I don't—"

"Or we could go down to the precinct," he told her evenly. "Your choice."

Kathy looked at her daughter, still clinging to her. She took a deep breath, making her decision. "My apartment."

"Good choice," Troy acknowledged. He glanced down at the terrified little girl. Taking a moment, he squatted down to Rachel's level. "Hi."

She stared at him with eyes that were the color of cornflowers, even in this light. "Hi."

"We just want to talk to your mom," he explained. "Is that all right with you?"

The little girl nodded.

Putting out his hand toward her, Troy waited until she was trusting enough to take it on her own. Which she did, albeit hesitantly. He rose again, still holding on to Rachel's hand.

"Let's go," he told the patrolman. "You take the lady's suitcase.

"I can carry it myself," she protested a bit too heatedly.

Troy's suspicions were aroused. He exchanged glances with Delene. The look in her eyes told him she was thinking exactly the same thing.

Delene fell into step before him while the patrolman "escorted" Kathy back into the apartment building. "You're good with kids," she noted, clearly surprised.

"Lots of kids in our family," he told her. Then he raised his brow at her, indicating the girl's hand. Delene understood. With a nod, she took the small hand from his.

"I'm Delene," she told the little girl. Rachel tried to pull her hand away. Delene pretended not to notice. "And you look sleepy."

The girl stopped tugging and stared up at her. "I am."

Stooping down, Delene picked her up in her arms. The child weighed less than a guilty conscience. "You're in luck. I love carrying sleepy girls."

Murmuring "Okay" against Delene's neck, the little girl curled up and promptly fell asleep in her arms.

The closer they got to her apartment, the more agitated Kathy became.

"I didn't do it," Kathy protested even before they reached her door. "I didn't do it," she cried even louder, as if pure volume would convince everyone and make them set her free.

"Didn't do what?" Troy asked innocently. He could see that the door to the apartment down the hall, was ajar.

Kathy was clearly upset. Had she not been flanked by the police, there was no doubt in Delene's mind that the younger woman would have bolted.

"I didn't kill him."

They'd reached Kathy's apartment. She'd left the door unlocked. He pushed it open, gesturing for her to enter—after the patrolman had gone in first.

"Who said anything about killing someone?" Troy asked.

"Nobody." Kathy began to fidget, running her hands up and down her arms the way someone did when they couldn't get warm.

Delene set the sleeping little girl down on the sofa.

Looking at Kathy, she felt for the younger woman. She knew terror when she saw it. And guilt. "Did you kill him?" she asked softly.

Kathy backed away. She might have kept going if the policeman hadn't blocked her way. *"No!"*

"But you have the gun," Delene assumed, her voice calm, nonaccusing.

"He gave it to me for protection," Kathy wailed, wringing her hands.

"Where is it?" Troy prodded.

Frantic, like a deer caught in the headlights of an oncoming car, Kathy's eyes moved from one face to another. "I don't know."

Toy looked over the suitcase the patrolman was still holding. "If I opened your suitcase, would I find it there?"

Kathy's breathing became audible. "You can't do that."

He wondered if it was just a desperate protest, or if the woman actually knew a little about the law.

"You're right, I can't. Why don't we just put it over there?" He indicated the shabby chair beside the sofa. The patrolman set it on the edge.

"Mind if I get some water?" Delene asked Kathy. Not waiting for a response, she turned and immediately bumped into the chair. The suitcase fell on the floor, its flimsy locks springing open. The contents of the case spilled out. Along with the gun she'd hidden inside. Delene looked down at the weapon almost at her feet. "Looks like that gun you don't remember misplacing crawled into your suitcase."

Troy took out a pen and slipped it through the trigger area, lifting the gun off the floor. For lack of an evidence bag, he carefully wrapped the weapon in his clean handkerchief. His eyes met Kathy's.

"I think that the bullet that killed Clyde came from this gun. What do you think?"

Instead of answering, Kathy covered her face with her hands and sank down on the floor. She began to sob. "He made me do it, he made me."

Handing the gun over to the patrolman, Troy moved forward until he was directly over her. "He said 'Kathy, please kill me'?"

She shook her head, then looked up, tearstains on her cheeks. "He said he'd take Rachel away. Clyde was a junkie. I've seen him when he's high—he doesn't know what he's doing. He would have sold Rachel for a fix and then not remember doing it." Kathy grew steadily more agitated. "I couldn't let that happen. I couldn't let him have her." She turned to Troy. "Don't you see? He gave me no choice."

He felt sorry for her. Really sorry. The one decent thing about her were her maternal instincts, but her way of life had trapped her.

"You know, in a strange sort of way, I understand," Troy told her. Very gently he took her arm and helped her up to her feet. "When you write it all down, put it just that way. That you were afraid of what he would do." Looking over toward the patrolman, he indicated that the man step forward. "Officer Ryan will take you down to the precinct."

Kathy stiffened as Ryan produced handcuffs and placed them on her wrists. She looked over toward the child sleeping on the sofa.

"But what about my daughter? If she gets into the system—" Her voice broke for a second, then returned, stronger than before. And filled with anxiety. "I know what happens in the system. I won't be able to get her back."

"Do you have any relatives?" Delene asked her. If worse came to worst, maybe she could take temporary custody of the little girl, she thought. "Someone you could leave her with?"

"I don't have—" Kathy began brokenly.

"I'll take her." They turned to see Louise Patton in the doorway. She was still wearing the same bold housecoat. She was also wearing a kindly expression. Stepping forward, she said to Kathy, "I raised two of my own. They're doing okay. I can look after Rachel until you know what's going on."

Pressing her lips together, Kathy nodded. "Thank you."

Troy nodded toward the officer to take the young woman away.

"She's going to need a good lawyer," Delene commented to Troy as he drove her back to her apartment. The patrolman had taken Kathy to the precinct, with instructions to remain with her until he could arrive. Troy had vetoed Delene's offer to accompany him. Delene knew it was against regulations, but she'd hoped they might be bent a little. They'd bent a lot of personal rules in the past few hours.

Daylight slowly moved in, sending the shadow of night on its way.

"I'll talk to my sister, see who she can recommend," he told her. They were less than a block away from her apartment. "Maybe she knows someone who's willing to take the case pro bono."

There was only a small chance of that, Delene thought. "I've got some money put away—"

He shook his head at the offer, amazed by the woman who made it. The cool, removed act was just that, he thought. An act. Beneath the bravado and tough words was a woman who cared. Maybe too much.

But that was all right, he thought. Given a choice, he'd rather she cared than not. "Let's see what I can do before you crack open your piggy bank."

Stopped at a light, Delene looked at him incredulously. Kathy was no one to him, just another "suspect."

"You'd do that for her?"

"Yes."

"Why?"

He wasn't used to explaining himself. People usually just let him do what needed doing without wanting the reasons behind it.

"Because she looks like she could use someone in her corner. And because I don't like the idea of a kid being put into the system if she has a mother who loves her." He turned the tables around. "You?"

"Same."

A woman of few words, he thought, amused. "I guess we're really not that different after all."

She saw the smile on his face and realized that it struck a chord within her. "Guess not."

Troy guided his vehicle into the apartment complex,

pulling into a vacant spot close to her door. "Congratu-
lations." He put out his hand.

She just looked at it for a second. "For what?"

She'd gotten so tangled in the woman's case, she'd
lost sight of the bigger picture. "You just solved Clyde's
murder."

The way she saw it, he'd solved it, not her. She'd
only been there because of the little girl. "Right back
at you." She grinned, putting her hand in his.

The next moment, he'd tugged her over to his side
of the vehicle. Before she could offer a protest about
the gearshift being an insurmountable obstacle, his
lips covered hers.

Chapter 14

The kiss deepened, threatening to spiral out of control if she didn't so something. Now.

"Mmmm."

The deeply appreciative sound seemed to escape from her of its own volition. At the last possible moment, before oblivion descended over her brain, Delene put her hands against his chest. With effort, she managed to wedge a place between them. Reluctantly she pulled her head back even though she wanted nothing more than to go on kissing him, to go on savoring this wildly exhilarating feeling that galloped through her veins.

Delene dragged in a lungful of air. "I've got to get ready for work. And you've got a 'suspect' to walk through the system," she reminded him when he was about to offer a protest.

"Right." Exhaling a deep sigh tinged with resignation, Troy sat back in his seat. His eyes swept over her face. Held her prisoner. "See you later?"

"We'll see." But even as she uttered the blasé phrase, she knew there wasn't a single damn blasé thing about her right now, not when it came to him. If Troy called back or appeared on her doorstep, she knew she'd be available. Because she wanted to be.

"What are you doing a week from this Saturday?"

One hand on the car handle, a hint of a smile graced her mouth. "I don't know. What am I doing a week from this Saturday?"

"My uncle's giving a party." To those who knew retired Chief of Police Andrew Cavanaugh, it was a fairly common statement. Not a month went by when there wasn't something Andrew felt needed celebrating, needed being commemorated by his cooking and the company of his family and friends. "It's one of the kids' birthdays," Troy told her, although even as he said it, he wasn't a hundred percent certain that was the reason behind the event, or if it was, which child would be blowing out candles. He didn't keep track of family birthdays the way Janelle did. "Why don't you come?"

Her eyes crinkled a little as the smile on her lips deepened. "Why don't you pick me up?"

He looked into her eyes and she felt her knees get weaker. "Done."

If she hadn't been holding on to the door handle,

she wouldn't have remembered that she needed to get out of the car.

This wasn't good, she told herself as she finally opened the door and got out. She should be retreating from Cavanaugh, not moving toward him. She didn't trust relationships, didn't trust her judgment when it came to them.

Reaching the stairwell, she turned. Troy waved to her before pulling away. Damn it, she was behaving like an adolescent. The last time she did that, it landed her in big trouble.

A movement out of the corner of her eye caught her attention, but when Delene turned to look, there was no one there. Even if there had been, so what? People lived here, for heaven's sake. People came and went. They lived. They moved. Why shouldn't she see something?

The shiver wouldn't release her, though, wouldn't go away.

She was letting her paranoia sprout again. But that was because for maybe the first time in a long time, she felt happy and that made her nervous. She didn't trust the feeling. Didn't trust it to remain.

Her trust had been MIA for so long, she wasn't sure if she would have been able to recognize what trust felt like even if she stumbled across it.

"It's really nice to meet you." The statement was uttered with effusion.

Before she could respond and say something along

the same lines, Delene found herself caught in a very warm embrace.

Andrew Cavanaugh, the former police chief of Aurora, was hugging her. After a beat, she returned the hug. The awkwardness she normally experienced at such contact was strangely absent. Andrew Cavanaugh made her feel at ease, as if he'd known her for a long time instead of just a few seconds.

Well, if nothing else, she was safe for a few hours, Delene thought in amusement as Andrew released her. Quickly scanning the living room she saw that there had to be at least eleven law-enforcement agents within a stone's throw. And that was only one room. The whole house and backyard seemed filled to capacity with people of all sizes and shapes, at least half of whom were with the police force.

Well, Troy had told her to brace herself when he'd rung the doorbell. She just hadn't realized how seriously he'd meant that warning.

Andrew Cavanaugh looked with approval at the young woman his youngest nephew had brought to his grandson's first birthday party. After some initial adjustments, she would fit right into their little family. There was a slightly wary look about her eyes and she gave him the impression she was on her guard against something, but that would pass in time.

Slipping his arm around her shoulders, Andrew inclined his head toward her ear and said, "Don't be afraid. The family tends to be overwhelming at first glance. At second and third, as well," he confessed, "but they're harmless and they grow on you."

She offered the man what she hoped passed for a smile. He was making it sound as if he expected her to be a returning guest. Her eyes shifted uncertainly toward Troy. Had he said something to the older man?

Taking his cue, Troy stepped up, gently extracting her from the man they all looked to as the family patriarch. "Don't scare her off, Uncle Andrew," he warned. "It took a lot of convincing to get Delene to come here and mingle with all of you in the first place."

Not a lot, Delene thought. Just very effective convincing. He'd laid his blueprints out the previous week. From the time he'd invited her to attend the party, he'd been coming over to her apartment every evening. Sunday, he turned up at ten in the morning. And stayed.

It had gotten to the point that she no longer involuntarily stiffened when she heard a knock on her door or the doorbell ring. Besides, she told herself, Russell wouldn't knock or ring. That kind of behavior was polite; it expressed a supplication to gain admittance. Russell didn't supplicate. He just barged in, as if he had a right to entrance. And to her.

Not anymore, she promised herself.

But she was thinking less and less of Russell these days and more and more about the man who made her heart skip several beats and her body heat by his very presence.

Though she refused to put it into so many words, deep down she knew she was moving on with her life.

Finally.

"Then we'll try to be worthy of the pleasure of her company," Andrew promised. Like a monarch who took pride in his kingdom, he looked out toward the throng. "Have the others met her yet?"

Just in case his uncle wanted to take it upon himself to do the honors, Troy took hold of Delene's arm. "Not yet."

Andrew stepped back, magnanimously gesturing toward the teeming room. "Then you'd better get to it."

As Troy began to walk to the heart of the living room, Delene turned her head toward him. "I've seen less people at *Star Trek* conventions."

He stopped to stare at her. "You go to *Star Trek* conventions?"

She didn't know if he was about to laugh at her or celebrate the fact. Either way, she could only tell him the truth. She shook her head. "No, but I've seen them on the news."

That made more sense. Try as he might, he couldn't picture her being impassioned about dilithium crystals. "Don't worry, there are no Klingons here." With effort, he bit back a laugh. "Although my brothers used to do a damn good imitation of Klingons during one of their numerous battles."

She had no idea what he was talking about, but she never got a chance to ask him to explain. One second they seemed to be on the outside fringe of the throng, the next, the throng had converged to swallow them up. She was surrounded by several tall, imposing men, each one handsomer than the last. And all of them bearing more than a fleeting resemblance to Troy.

"Hi, I'm Dax." Bright blue eyes flashed at her, accompanying a Troyesque grin as Dax extended his hand to her.

At the same moment, another hand crossed over his, taking hers as a second dark-haired, blue-eyed man, slightly shorter than Dax, said, "I'm Jared."

"My brothers," Troy explained. There was no missing the affection despite the frown that graced his lips. "And these two Neanderthals—" he continued as two more joined the number "—are my cousins Shaw and Clay. Uncle Andrew's sons."

Shaw smiled at her while his younger brother grinned and nodded his head in approval. "Nice," he told Troy.

"They'll engulf you if you're not careful." The warning came from directly behind her, delivered by yet another dark-haired man who could have been a dead ringer for Troy.

She felt a little like someone who had fallen headlong into a Xerox machine and kept seeing nothing but copies all around her.

With a sigh, Troy inclined his head toward the newest arrival. "And this is Patrick."

"Are you Chief Andrew Cavanaugh's son, too?" she asked.

Patrick's smile was ever so slightly more sensitive than the ones that graced his cousins' lips. She had the feeling that Patrick Cavanaugh was less gregarious than the others. "No, my dad was Mike Cavanaugh."

Another new name. Delene raised a brow as she looked back at Troy.

"I'll have a score card made up for you," Troy promised as he extracted her from the center of the growing mob scene.

"You should have made up flash cards for me before we got here," she told him. He'd mentioned names, but she hadn't actually processed just how many cousins he had. And that didn't even begin taking in the spouses. "How do you keep everyone straight?"

Stopping at the open bar, he paused to pour her a glass of white wine. He handed it off to her, then took a bottle of beer for himself.

"I never really thought about it," he confessed. By the time he was born, all his cousins were already there. He grinned at her. "I guess I've always had an eye for faces."

She took a sip of her wine, then raised her eyes to his face. "And figures?" she guessed.

His expression belonged to a man whose soul was innocent. "Not me."

Had she been drinking, she would have choked. "Oh, must have been another Troy Cavanaugh I heard those stories about."

Had she been investigating him the way he'd tried to do with her? Was her interest in him that aroused? He certainly hoped so. "What stories?"

Jorge, who had several relatives on the Aurora police force himself, had brought the stories to her as if they were a basket of apples, each to be digested. "The ones that say you go through women like most people go through clean shirts."

He raised his free hand as if he was taking a solemn oath. "I don't send them to the cleaners to be pressed." And then his expression softened. "And I've had a great many rewarding, good relationships."

Well, at least he didn't lie. But was he bragging? "I bet you had."

He set the beer bottle down on the table, his attention fixed only on her. "Right now," his fingertips lightly touched the tips of her hair, "I can't remember a single name, a single face." For him, the room had melted away. "Just you."

She had to remind herself to breathe. And to lock her knees in place because if she didn't, she just might slide down to the floor. "And if I fell for that?" she asked in a whisper.

His eyes held hers. "Nothing to fall for. Just stating a fact."

Disregarding the fact that he was standing in the middle of his uncle's house and that at least twenty people in the immediate vicinity were bearing witness, he kissed her. Lightly enough not to draw comment, deeply enough to tell her that he was serious.

"So, have you met her yet?" Rayne Cavanaugh, Andrew's youngest daughter, asked Janelle. The two were catching up, nursing drinks less than ten feet away from Delene and Troy.

Troy had mentioned the woman once or twice, not enough to alert her, only to make her familiar with the name. "This is the first time I've gotten a look at her." Toying with her rum and Coke, Janelle studied her youngest older brother. Pieces of previous conversations began to fall into place for her. Watching him now with Delene, she got a definite feeling that this woman was not like the others. "You notice something different about Troy?"

Rayne cocked her head, looking at Troy, trying to discern her cousin's meaning. "Different how?"

Janelle shrugged. Usually words came easily to her. But not this time. "I don't know, just different. He's always been attentive to any woman he's brought to one of these functions, but there's just something about the way he touches Delene's elbow, something about the way he looks at her...."

Rayne heard what wasn't being said. "Think he's finally getting serious?"

Janelle laughed softly as she shook her head. The last male Cavanaugh was being struck down. Who would have ever thought?

"I didn't think it was possible, but yes. Maybe." She sighed. "If he is falling for her, that woman had better be good to him." She downed the rest of her drink, then set down the chunky glass on the first available surface. "Otherwise, I'll have to kill her."

"That would certainly go a long way toward spoiling her day," Rayne commented.

Janelle laughed. "Not to mention mine. Murder doesn't look good on an assistant district attorney's résumé. C'mon, I need a refill."

Rayne looked down at her glass. It was all but empty. "Yeah, me, too." Just then her husband approached. "And here's my refill now," she cracked.

"I think she's already had her limit, Cole," Janelle told the man who came to join them. "I'd watch her if I were you."

Cole nuzzled his wife's neck. "With pleasure."

Troy held his peace as long as he could. Though he didn't talk about it, his family was very precious to him and for the first time since he could remember, approval was actually an issue. He'd seen theirs by the way they acted.

Hers, however, remained a mystery.

"So, what did you think?"

It had been a long party. And she had enjoyed every minute because never once had they made her feel like an outsider. Delene was leaning back in the passenger seat, having set it to a semi-inclined position. She'd kicked off her shoes the second she'd gotten into his car.

"I'm not sure I can think. My head's still humming. Not to mention that my feet are aching." She thought about massaging them, but they hurt so much she didn't even want to touch them. "I don't think I've *ever* spent that many hours in high heels."

She was diverting the conversation, but he decided he'd let her. She *looked* as if she'd enjoyed herself. "You could have taken them off at any time. Uncle Andrew's not a stickler for formality."

She looked at him as if he'd just suggested she go skinny dipping in the punch bowl. "No way. If I took off my shoes, I would have been trampled on. Everyone there was taller than I was, including some of the five-year-olds."

Taking the last turn to her apartment complex, he grinned. "I didn't know you had this penchant for exaggeration."

Neither did she. Today had been a very different, very nice experience for her. She'd never been at a family gathering before. Birthdays when she was growing up were solitary affairs, just her mother and her. When her mother remembered that it *was* her birthday.

"A lot of things about me that you don't know," she replied, doing her very best to create an aura of mystery.

Night traveled along with them on their way back to her apartment, darkening the windows. Turning her head, Delene caught her reflection in the side window.

She was smiling.

For no reason.

When was the last time that had happened?

The last time she was with Troy. The man had a way of bringing out the smiles that were deeply embedded inside of her.

You're getting carried away, a small voice in her

head warned, not for the first time. That same small, practical voice that had urged her to make good her escape from Russell. The voice of reason.

"So tell me," Troy urged as he stopped behind a battered Volvo, waiting for the light to change.

She looked at him, confused. "Tell you what?"

"If there are all these 'mysterious' things about you that I still don't have a clue about, tell me what they are." He turned to look at her. "I'm listening."

The smile on her lips faded. He was digging. To possess her? "I didn't mean—"

Glancing, he saw that the light had turned green again. The Volvo in front of them had begun to move. And so did he. His hands tightened slightly on the steering wheel, but his expression never wavered. Never gave her a clue about what he was feeling inside.

"Okay," he allowed, forcing his voice to sound cheerful, "too soon. I can accept that. Maybe later."

"Later as in later tonight?"

"No, as in later-later." He glanced at Delene. Despite all her bravado, she still spooked easily. The last thing he wanted was to spook her. "Tomorrow. Next week. Next month."

Even as Troy said the words, he realized that he meant them. Without thinking about it, he'd made plans. Plans for them. Plans about their future. A future he wanted to spend together.

Wow, when had that happened? When had he gone from Troy Cavanaugh, lover of women, to Troy Cavanaugh, lover of *the* woman? All he could conclude was that it had just snuck up on him somewhere during the night.

Beside him, Delene was stiffening. He drew the only logical conclusion that he could. "I'm scaring you, aren't I?"

She didn't understand. How did he know her that well? Was that just a lucky guess? They had hardly been together at all. How did he see into her soul with such clarity? Because she'd felt that he had that ability all along, that's how. She couldn't be anything less than honest with him. "Yes."

He wished it were otherwise. But some things took time. A smile flashed quickly, curving and then releasing his lips. "Sorry, didn't mean to. We can take this slow. This is new for me, too." The confession was an afterthought.

She laughed shortly. "What, seducing a woman?"

"No, *that* I've been doing for a long time," he said with no fanfare, no vanity at all. "I mean making plans with the woman I've seduced—real plans," he emphasized. And then, to keep the moment from becoming too serious, he grinned. "And, as I remember it, you were the one who extended the invitation first, not the other way around so technically," he concluded, driving into her apartment complex, "you seduced me."

She hadn't meant it that way. She'd just wanted to get all the sexual tension behind her so that she could think clearly. And now she couldn't seem to think clearly at all. "Troy."

He heard so much in her voice. The note of pleading.

The request for indulgence. That was when he realized that he loved her. And if she needed all this, okay, so be it. He cared enough to step back.

The regular spots in guest parking were full. There were a lot of overnight guests parking tonight. He wouldn't be one of them. "You want me to let you have your space, is that it?"

What was this strange ache in her heart? When had she started caring? Why would she do that to herself?

She avoided his eyes. "Yes."

"Space is another word for vacant. Nobody wants to feel vacant, Delene. To feel empty." Finally finding a place, he brought the car to a stop. But he didn't cut off the engine. "I know I don't and I don't think that you do, either." He made one attempt at convincing her before he backed off. "Don't let what happened to you five years ago rob you of being happy. Because then he's won and you've lost."

She sighed. Everything felt so mixed-up inside her head. "You're making sense. You're being logical. But in here—" she tapped her head "—I still can't help being afraid."

"It's not a battle you should face by yourself." But he didn't want her to think he was pressuring her, so he leaned over and kissed her lightly on the lips. "But okay, I'll let you spend the night without me. Absence makes the heart grow fonder, they tell me. You'd better grow a lot fonder," he told her. "Because what I had planned for tonight…"

Delene put her fingertips across his lips, not wanting to hear. Not wanting to be tempted. "Rain check," she said.

"Haven't you heard? It never rains in California," he reminded her. "Want me to walk you to your door?" From where he parked, he would have to crane his neck to see her go in.

She shook her head. "I'll be all right." And then she paused for a second. "Diane," she told him. "It's Diane."

They'd just taken another giant step forward, he thought. "Your name?" She nodded. "Diane," he repeated. "It's very pretty."

She said nothing. Quickly she got out of the car. Before she begged him to spend the night.

She knew she needed time. Time to sort this out. Time to think. And she couldn't think when he was around. Because all she wanted to do was make love with him.

With quick steps, she hurried up the stone stairs leading to her loft. Unlocking the door, she hesitated before stepping inside. The loneliness was already beginning to engulf her. She thought about running down the stairs again and trying to catch him. With effort, she forced herself to walk into her apartment.

She closed the door behind her, turned and faced...

"Hello, Diane. Have a nice evening?"

Russell was sitting on her sofa.

Chapter 15

Delene couldn't move.

At first she was certain she was having another nightmare. She'd visualized Russell coming back into her life so many times, in so many different ways, that for a brief moment, she clung to the scrap of hope that she was hallucinating.

He couldn't actually be here. He just couldn't.

Russell's lips slowly peeled back from his perfect, white teeth. The smile on his face was positively feral. It made her blood run cold. And begin pumping double-time in her veins.

Delene remained where she stood, wondering how long it would take him to catch up to her if she turned around and ran. She was faster than he was, but his legs were longer.

And then anger set in. How dare he be here? After everything he'd done to her, how dare he show up and invade her life like this?

"Get out of here, Russell."

Anger flashed across Russell's suntanned, smooth brow. The next moment, it disappeared again without a trace. Delene remembered that he was at his worst when he appeared deadly calm.

"Quite a life you've carved out for yourself, Diane." The deep, resonant voice that echoed through so many courtrooms filled her tiny apartment, oppressing her. Mocking her.

She rallied as if her life depended on it. Because it did. "I'm not the frightened nineteen-year-old you could use as a punching bag anymore."

He seemed not to hear her. Instead, still sitting on the sofa, he steepled his fingers before him as he regarded her. His gaze was intense. It took effort not to shift uncomfortably.

"I don't like the clothing," he finally said, nodding at the outfit she was wearing, "but you've filled out. Blossomed."

She wasn't interested in his stamp of approval, or what he thought of her after all this time. She just wanted him out of here, out of her life. "We're not married anymore, Russell. You have no right to be here if I don't want you to be."

Russell seemed to struggle with his temper. "Don't talk to me about rights, Diane," he told her smoothly. "You're way out of your league. That cheap Mexican divorce isn't worth the paper it's printed on. I can have it rescinded anytime I want."

She was smarter now than when she'd married him. Could think on her feet. The fact that he hadn't had the divorce rescinded told her that it wasn't as easily managed as he claimed.

With all her heart, she wished she had her gun in her hands. But it hadn't seemed right, dropping it into her purse and bringing it to a family party. There was no need for it with all those law-enforcement agents around. There was a need for it now.

She remained firm. Any displays of weakness would have him going for the jugular. "I don't want to debate you, Russell, I just want you gone."

"Not without you, Diane." She saw the rage he was fighting to keep from exploding. "You shamed me, embarrassed me in front of my friends, my employer."

His employer. The man responsible for who knew how many ruined lives, not to mention dead people. She sneered at him. "Oh, right, and the head of a crime family has such high standards." Her hand on the doorknob, she was about to pull it open. "Get out, Russell. Get out before I call the police."

What he said next froze her in her tracks far more effectively than anything he could have possibly done to her. "What, you mean your boyfriend? Think he can help you?" He rose, a menacing figure in a three-thousand-dollar gray Versace suit. "Think again."

Was he bluffing? Not even Russell would go up

against an entire law-enforcement family. "What do you know about him?"

She tried not to shiver when she saw his smile widen. "I always do my homework, you know that. And I know a lot, oh love of my life. For instance, I know that you've turned into a whore, disgracing your marriage vows."

Something inside her snapped. If anyone had disgraced their marriage vows, he had. He'd promised to love, to cherish and to protect her. Using his fists to put her in a coma did none of those.

"We are not married," she said in between clenched teeth.

He seemed to grow in stature right before her eyes. "We're married if I say we're married," he told her malevolently.

She took her stand. The way she should have done years ago. "I'm not going back with you. I'd rather die first."

He laughed. The sound cut straight to the bone. Anger flared within her again, smothering the fear that had been steadily rising inside her breast.

"That can be arranged." Rising to his feet, he began to circle around her, a predator toying with his prey, trying to decide whether to kill it now or at some later point. "But not before you watch that fine young police detective of yours die a slow, painful death." His eyes locked on hers. "Don't think I wouldn't do it. Maybe I'll even throw in a few members of his family, as well. No extra charge." He grabbed her by the shoulders, rage flaring in his eyes. "You know me, Diane. You know that I don't make empty threats." He released her, the cold smile back on his lips. "Now, what'll it be? Will you come back with me peacefully, or do I have to eliminate that pretty detective of yours?" He lowered his head. "And I guarantee you, he won't be pretty when I finish. He'll be begging for me to put an end to his misery. And cursing you with his dying breath."

He'd drawn her a dramatic scenario, but she didn't doubt that it was also true. Every word of it. She had no reason to doubt him. However long it took to fulfill his promise, she knew Russell wouldn't deviate from the course.

She would never be able to breathe easily. And, more important, neither would Troy or any of his family. She couldn't be responsible for that. Her own life she was more than willing to risk, but not theirs.

She knew what she had to do.

Something inside of her died.

"All right." Her own voice sounded hollow to her. "I'll go back with you. As long as I have your word that you won't harm any of them."

"Still the bleeding heart. Nice to know that some things don't change. Don't worry, I have no desire for a bloodbath." Russell deliberately smirked at her. "All I want is what's mine."

Delene took a breath. What was his, she knew, was revenge, and there was no doubt in her mind that he would exact it, perhaps even kill her.

But death was preferable to being his wife. And all that really mattered to her was that Troy was safe.

It was at that moment she realized just how much Troy had come to mean to her.

She loved him.

She couldn't lose that, something inside of her cried frantically.

She needed to stall, to think. There *had* to be a way out of this. A way to keep Russell from dragging her back. She began to cross toward the closet. "I'll just throw some things together—"

Catching her by the arm, Russell jerked her to him. "Leave everything here," he ordered. "It's all just cheap trash anyway. There's nothing you have here that I can't buy for you."

She raised her head defiantly, looking directly into his dark eyes. Russell was wrong. He couldn't begin to buy or replace what she was leaving behind. Because she was leaving behind her heart, her happiness.

But that was because she had to. Troy would be dead within hours if she didn't.

"All right," she agreed with resignation framed in hatred. And then, because she just had to know how she'd slipped up, she asked, "How did you find me?"

The smirk reappeared, as if to mock her ever thinking that she could get away. "I didn't. Santangelo did. He was here on business, actually." He left the details nebulous. He never talked about his employer's affairs. "He was watching the news when he saw someone he thought looked like you. So he called me. I told him to make sure and call me when he was. He did."

The news. That awful cameraman outside of Clyde's motel room—*he* was to blame for all this.

And then she realized that she hadn't been wrong, hadn't been imagining it. There *had* been someone following her.

God, she wished she had acted on that suspicion instead of shrugging it off to paranoia.

Just because you're paranoid doesn't mean they're not after you, she thought cynically.

Suddenly anxious to get going, Russell snapped. "Enough talk. Let's go!"

Just as he took hold of her arm, there was a knock on the door. He looked at Delene accusingly. "The second shift?" he asked insultingly.

She was just waiting to get an unobstructed shot at him. To throw him on the ground and make him feel helpless, as helpless as she'd felt when his fists were pummeling her, "I don't know who that is."

The second knock was more urgent. "Impatient," Russell observed. "You must have gotten better in bed than I remember."

She hated the way he invaded her life, making everything she'd had with Troy seem so dirty. "If I did, it was because I had something better to work with."

Uttering a curse, he raised his hand to hit her. Then, as if he realized that was what she wanted, that she had probably learned how to use his anger, not to mention his size, against him, Russell dropped his hand.

The third knock was harder still. "Open it," he ordered.

But even as she moved to do so, Russell moved with her, his fingers wrapped around her upper arm. He wasn't about to let her go free, not even for a second.

Troy blew out a breath. Where *was* she? The loft wasn't big enough for her not to hear him. Had she decided to go out? To take a walk in order to clear her head?

He'd promised himself to stay away, at least for the night. He'd tried to convince himself that what she said was true. She needed her space. He'd almost gotten all the way home before he decided that she'd had space for five years; now she was going to have something to fill that space.

For once in his life he wasn't going to remain laid-back, he was going to push. Push in order to make her see just what she meant to him. He had to convince her through words, not silence, that he could give her a life that would make her forget everything that had come before.

When she didn't answer on the third knock, he gave serious thought to picking the lock. And then the door opened.

"Hi, I—"

All the words he'd rehearsed dried on his lips the moment he saw that there was someone else in the room with her.

He felt like an idiot. Here he was, making plans and she'd had someone else all along.

No, that wasn't her. Delene wasn't capable of that kind of deception. Not the woman he'd been with. He wasn't, nor had he ever been, a poor judge of character. Certainly not as poor as that.

He turned his attention away from the man and toward Delene. "Did I come at a bad time?"

Russell tightened his hold on her arm. The smile on his lips was steely.

"That all depends on your point of view," he told Troy. "If you're here to have sex with my wife, I'd say that you came at a very bad time. Matter of fact, there would never be a good time for that."

"Your wife?" Troy echoed. He looked incredulously at Delene. Was this her ex? All she'd ever said about him was that he was charming. This guy wasn't charming, he was a jerk.

"Tell him, honey," Russell urged. He deliberately nuzzled her, never taking his eyes off the man by the door. Wanting to see his reaction. Wanting to goad him. "Tell him about how you decided to skip out on me when things didn't go your way. Tell him how worried I've been about you. How I spent over a hundred thousand dollars trying to find you." His expression mocked Troy. "Tell him how you're going back with me."

Why was she just standing there, taking this? Did he have a weapon he was holding trained on her? Troy looked, but there was no indication that she was being held against her will.

"Delene?"

She bit her lip. For his sake, she had to lie, she told herself. She didn't want him following her. Didn't want him getting hurt or, God forbid, killed on her account.

Her expression was stoic, distant, as she said, "He's telling you the truth, Troy. I've decided to go back with Russell."

He didn't believe her. She wasn't doing this of her own free will. Not after what she'd told him about the man she'd been married to. He looked into her eyes, searching for a sign. They were lifeless.

There was only a shell of a person standing before him now.

Troy took a step toward her. "You're not going anywhere with him."

"Don't start something you have no hope of finishing, Detective," Russell warned him malevolently.

Troy's eyes met his. "I'm not," he answered evenly. "I have every intention of finishing this." He played for time, hoping to get the man off guard. "For all I know, you're not even her husband."

"I'm her husband," Russell told him. The edge that came into his voice would have sent those who knew him running for cover.

She wanted Troy out of harm's way. "Troy, please—"

But his attention was on the man with Delene. "I'm going to need some ID."

Russell sneered. "Okay, have it your way, pretty boy. It's in my pocket."

But instead of the wallet Troy thought he was going to take out, Russell pulled out a gun.

Delene's heart leaped into her throat. She knew what Russell was like. He would give the selection of his socks in the morning more thought than he would allocate to whether or not he should shoot Troy where he stood.

The second she saw the gun, she screamed, "No!" and grabbed his arm with both hands. Delene screamed a second time when the gun discharged. A bullet tore through her flesh.

"You bitch!" Russell shouted.

White rage exploded in Troy's veins. He hardly remembered what happened next. Flying at Russell, he knocked the other man down on the floor. The gun flew out of Russell's hand and landed just out of reach as they fought one another.

For a split second, they seemed almost evenly matched. Russell was taller, heavier, but Troy was younger, trained and right now completely incensed with a fury that gave him extraordinary strength while cutting away his pain factor to almost nothing. Each landed blows while struggling to reach the gun on the floor. When Russell finally managed to grab it, Troy tackled him and they both went down.

The weapon discharged for a second time. And for a second time, it hit flesh. As Delene watched in horror, Russell scrambled to his feet.

He'd killed Troy was all she could think. And now she was going to kill him.

But then, his eyes wide with disbelief, Russell clutched the front of his chest and looked down. Blood oozed between his fingers. He couldn't stop it, couldn't make it go back.

Sinking to his knees as he cursed the wild shot, Russell fell face forward.

His eyes trained on the other man's prone figure, Troy rushed over to Delene. Weak, stunned and shaken, she was attempting to struggle to her feet. She was pressing her palm against her left shoulder.

Releasing it, she touched Troy, looking for signs of a hole. There were none. Tears filled her eyes. "Are you all right?" she cried, her voice cracking.

He pointed out the absurdity of the question. "I'm the only one in the room who hasn't been shot." Quickly examining her, he saw that the wound was not as serious as he'd first thought. She was, however, losing a lot of blood. Her face was paler than he'd ever seen it. "The bullet went clean through."

She didn't hear him. Her eyes were on the man lying close by. He wasn't moving. Was that just to catch them off guard? Or was it all finally over?

"Is he...?"

Troy left her side. Cautiously he stooped over the lawyer's body and felt the side of Russell's neck. There was nothing. Troy looked up at Delene. "He's not going to be bothering you anymore."

Finally. She was finally free.

It was only then that she became aware of the moisture on her cheeks.

She was crying.

* * *

"Hell of a night, Troy," Brian commented to his son, placing a hand on his shoulder in silent support.

They were standing right outside the hospital lounge where friends and family of patients waited to receive official word about the outcome of a surgery.

There was a small chapel located to one side, but it was filled. Troy preferred to do his praying silently, away from any outward religious trappings.

Andrew pretended to laugh shortly. "I'll say this, you sure know how to cap off a party."

Both men had come, along with several of his cousins, both of his brothers as well as Janelle and a few assorted in-laws, as soon as they had heard about the incident. Word had reached them the second he had called Dispatch to get an ambulance and one of the medical examiners to the scene.

By the time they'd reached the hospital, Delene had lost consciousness. She was taken into surgery almost immediately. He'd stopped breathing around the same time.

Coming over to join them, Dax gave his younger brother an encouraging smile. "Don't worry, bro. She's going to be all right."

"Yeah," Jared chimed in, approaching from the other direction. "If she can put up with you, she can handle anything."

His nerves were at the edge of endurance. Delene had been shot trying to save him. Why hadn't he gone in with her in the first place? Why had he just let her walk off like that? He gave Jared an impatient look. "Is this your idea of being supportive?"

"Pretty much," Janelle told him, coming out of the chapel to join the others. "You know they were all raised in a cave." She flashed a smile at him, a smile that told him everything would turn out all right. "Except for me, of course."

"You?" Dax hooted. "You're the worst of us all. Why—"

The teasing abruptly halted as a heavyset surgeon dressed in green scrubs came through the double doors that separated Operating Room One from the rest of the hospital. He looked tired, but pleased.

Troy was the first to reach him.

Out of respect for their nerves and because he was tired, the surgeon gave them the short version. "She's going to be fine." He looked at the only man with blood on his shirt and made the correct assessment. "You're Troy, right?" Troy nodded, not quite trusting his own voice yet. "She's asking for you. Only a few minutes," he cautioned. "She needs her rest." He pointed to a set of doors beside the operating room. "Recovery's right through there."

"Give her our love, boy," Andrew said, patting him on the back to send him on his way.

"Remember, you can't give her your own until she's well enough," Clay called after him.

Troy only heard voices, not words. His attention was fixed on getting to Delene's side. Everything else was secondary.

* * *

She looked frail and small in the hospital bed, he thought when he finally approached Delene.

His heart tightened in his chest.

If that bullet had been just a few inches to the right, then she would have been...

He shut the thought from his mind, unable to even complete it.

She turned her head toward him just before he reached her. "Hi," she said weakly.

He took her right hand in his, needing to touch her, to feel that she was warm and alive instead of cold.

"Hi," he echoed. He struggled for breath, feeling like a man who had been on the marathon run of his life. "The doctor says you're going to be all right."

"I am." She smiled weakly. "Now that you're here." Her eyes felt very heavy, but there were things she had to know. Things she had to hear now, in order to find peace. "Did I imagine it? Is he really dead?"

Still holding her hand, Troy smiled. "Coroner seems to think so. They took him away in a body bag. You're free now, Delene." Emotion choked him. It could have so easily gone otherwise. "Free to live your life any way you want to." He pressed a kiss to her hand. "I'm hoping that you want to live it with me."

She looked at him, having only enough strength to raise one corner of her mouth in a smile. "Not when all you want to kiss is my hand." She took a deep breath, then another, before continuing. "What made you come back?"

Luck. And a surge of stubbornness, he thought now. "I wanted to propose."

"Propose?" Her head was swimming. He couldn't mean what she thought he did. "Propose what?"

"Marriage."

She blinked. Was she dreaming? No, her body ached too much for this to be a dream. "To me?"

He laughed. "Well, it wouldn't have been to your ex."

He was going to propose. To her. The words replayed themselves in her head several times, bringing a little more joy with them each time.

She had to know. "What were you going to say?"

Troy took a breath, as if preparing, then said, "I was going to say, 'Will you marry me?'"

She blinked, waiting. "And that's all?"

"Why?" He grinned at her. Only Delene would argue about the length of a proposal. "Isn't that enough?"

She thought about it for a moment. "Seeing as how it's you, yes, it's enough."

It was his turn to wait. In vain. Maybe this was going too fast for her, he thought. He didn't want her to think he was crowding her. "You can have all the time you want to think about it."

A little of her old spirit was making a comeback. "I don't need any time to think about it. I already know what my answer is going to be." She smiled, both sides of her mouth now curving. "Yes. My answer's yes. Provided that you kiss something other than my hand to seal the bargain."

Kneeling beside her bed, Troy bent over and very lightly kissed her lips.

"Better," she murmured. "Much better." Her eyes crinkled as she looked at him. "Do it again."

And he did.

* * * * *

FAMOUS FAMILIES

YES! Please send me the *Famous Families* collection featuring the Fortunes, the Bravos, the McCabes and the Cavanaughs. This collection will begin with 3 FREE BOOKS and 2 FREE GIFTS in my very first shipment— and more valuable free gifts will follow! My books will arrive in 8 monthly shipments until I have the entire 51-book *Famous Families* collection. I will receive 2-3 free books in each shipment and I will pay just $4.49 U.S./$5.39 CDN for each of the other 4 books in each shipment, plus $2.99 for shipping and handling.* If I decide to keep the entire collection, I'll only have paid for 32 books because 19 books are free. I understand that accepting the 3 free books and gifts places me under no obligation to buy anything. I can always return a shipment and cancel at any time. My free books and gifts are mine to keep no matter what I decide.

268 HCN 9971   468 HCN 9971

Name _____ (PLEASE PRINT) _____

Address _____ Apt. # _____

City _____ State/Prov. _____ Zip/Postal Code _____

Signature (if under 18, a parent or guardian must sign)

Mail to the **Reader Service**:

IN U.S.A.: P.O. Box 1867, Buffalo, NY 14240-1867
IN CANADA: P.O. Box 609, Fort Erie, Ontario L2A 5X3

ReaderService.com

Manage your account online!

- Review your order history
- Manage your payments
- Update your address

> ### *We've designed the Reader Service website just for you.*

Enjoy all the features!

- Reader excerpts from any series
- Respond to mailings and special monthly offers
- Discover new series available to you
- Browse the Bonus Bucks catalogue
- Share your feedback

Visit us at:
ReaderService.com